# A DESIRE TO BE ALIVE

## A DESIRE
### BOOK TWO

## IVORY RAVEN

LJ MARSHALL'S
PUBLISHING HOUSE

ISBN: 979-8-9914097-5-9

ISBN: 979-8-9914097-4-2 (e-book)

Published by LJ Marshall's Publishing House
An imprint of Aoshiki Press

# CONTENTS

# PROLOGUE

No matter how far you run away from it, fate will always catch on. I always thought of myself as an above average man with an average dream to be free. A man who once sought freedom. I tried to mess with my fate and failed. The consequences were tougher than what I expected. Losing both the ones you loved and hated; I guess it's the balance of life. Ever since Anna left me alone, I felt strange feelings. A combination of soreness and some feelings I couldn't express in words. Her death changed my life dramatically. I experienced depression more than usual; guilt wrapped my heart just like a piece of candy. Once you unwrap it, you can taste its core. But, as long as it's wrapped, you will only have your imagination to guess what is hidden beneath the wrap.

Understanding emotions wasn't one of my strengths. I've always lived for me, and only me. What's the point of connecting your feelings to a mortal who could easily cut himself loose? My parents set all their hopes in raising me as the face of the family; in a matter of weeks, I crushed their desperate dreams. I thought Anna was special; 'the one', if you will. The moment I realized her importance in my life, she vanished leaving nothing but her golden glasses. I lost hope in love. Even my mom, a person who I admired for a long time, turned against me. She was a woman who walked behind money. Instead of helping people, she used her psychological knowledge to get what her heart desires. I made an oath the day Anna died; a principle I had to keep in order to survive. 'Never trust anybody...'

Each human has something that another human wants. She will allure him, and he will allure her. After getting what they wanted, the other person will be dumped for the dogs to play with. What's so great about love anyway? Don't these people know that their 'significant other' is just in for something?

I wonder if those thoughts will ever change. Or is it just the truth I wanted to avoid? I feel dizzy, maybe from those anti-depression pills. I want to sleep; good night, Anna...

# VISIT

"I'm awake, I was just resting my eyes…"

After Michael returned to Dubai, Lucas applied for a scholarship to study with him. He was a semester late but caught up with the rest. It's been almost a year since they had buried Anna. The summer vacation began last week; and both headed back to Los Angeles. Dubai in summer is a gamble for most of those who lived their lives in colder areas; you either survive it or escape it. Michael adjusted his seat to its default position and shoved the book into the backpack. People stood up to get their bags the moment the plane touched the ground. Michael and Lucas remained silent in their seats. A few minutes later, the plane was deserted, except for the flight attendance and them.

"Michael!" waved David.

Both forced themselves through the crowds until they reached the excited David. "I couldn't tell it was you with that beard," he chuckled, while placing both suitcases on the trolley thing he brought.

"Since Anna wasn't around, I felt that I don't need to take

care about shaving my beard. Also, people in Dubai appreciate a guy with a beard." remarked Michael. "Does mom or Isabella know you came here?" he then inquired.

"No, I did as you said and drove early. I'm almost certain both were soundly asleep. I told the other butlers to cover for me," David explained.

Lucas offered Michael to live with him. Michael didn't want to bother Richard; and he didn't want to return home. He gratefully accepted Lucas' offer, and they both arrived at his house after a thirty-minute drive. "Do you want me to wait here?" asked David.

"It's all right, I'll be staying here. Thanks for picking us up," Michael said.

"I'm glad you're doing fine. See you soon, Michael," he smiled, then drove back to the Walker's Mansion.

Lucas showed Michael to the guest room, then hurried to surprise his still sleeping parents. Meanwhile Michael sat his luggage and waited outside for Lucas. They both wanted to visit Anna first thing after arriving. Soon, Michael heard a car starting; he turned around but find no one inside.

"Hey, buddy!" called Lucas as he just exited the front door.

"How did you do that?"

"Newer cars have this feature where you can start them from distance. Cool isn't it?" Michael nodded in agreement.

Lucas drove to the cemetery, and Michael felt a huge pain in his chest. It was a mixture of guilt for Anna's death; and happiness of being able to see her again after a long semester. As they walked by the tombstones, Lucas stopped. "Isn't this your father's?" he asked, flicking his eyes Michael's way.

"Yes," Michael sighed.

"Won't you at least say hi to him? Are you just gonna ignore his existence as a soul?"

"What's the point? He's just a pile of bones now. Plus, I

didn't care about his existence as a living human being, what makes you think I'd care now?" Michael spoke of what he was thinking of at that very moment. For him, Larry was the reason for his life to turn upside down. He was the marionette that used to control Michael's strings.

A few tombstones later, they finally arrived at Anna's. Michael's heart pounded; faster and harder than when he would think about her. He still couldn't believe she was dead; that she was no longer there with them. She was basically living in a different place; a mysterious dimension that once you enter, you can't return to tell the tales. Both sat down near her tombstone. Michael closed his eyes, and flashbacks started to appear in his mind. Those couple of months he knew Anna had a lot of memories. Good and bad—but mostly good.

"Michael? Is that you?" Michael turned around to see Richard walking towards them. "Hey, Richard. Nice to see you again," Richard hugged him; and Michael wasn't sure how to react in such situations, so he simply hugged him back. Richard then sat with them near Anna's tombstone. They talked about random stuff. He asked about university; and they asked him about his job.

"All right, we have to go now," remarked Lucas. Michael stood up and eyed Richard one last time; he knew Richard wanted to have a private moment with his daughter. His chest echoed with pain, and Michael could feel his heart dancing in its place. "Richard, I'm sorry for Anna," he at last said.

Richard smiled back, "It's all right."

On their way to the car, Michael stopped midway, "Lucas, can you go ahead? I'll be right back. I just… I wanna check something."

"All right, I'll wait in the car."

Michael hurried back to Larry's grave. He gazed at the

tombstone, and Larry's image popped up in his head. "I honestly don't know what to think of you. Should I call you 'father', or perhaps 'master'?" Michael muttered, "While you ruined my childhood, you also sheltered me. You took care of my basic needs. But then, that was what a puppet master would do. Either way, I hope your soul can rest in peace," he paused for a while. "I'm not sure you can see, but tears are coming out for someone like you; can you believe that?"

Michael returned to Lucas some five minutes later. "You did the right thing," noted Lucas with a bright smile up his face.

"What are you talking about?"

"Never mind." Lucas drove with a subtle chuckle.

THE MONTH WENT BY FAST, and it was time to head back; Michael and Lucas passed by Anna's grave before arriving at the Los Angelus International Airport. David had to drive, even though he was disappointed that Michael didn't visit his own home. The two shared an apartment in Dubai. The location was good, and so were the neighbors. Michael dropped his luggage and went directly to bed. They arrived around nine in the evening; and after reaching the apartment, it was already past ten. "Don't forget your pills," remarked Lucas.

Depression has not left Michael's side since Anna's death. His therapist, Thomas, prescribed antidepressants to help with the problem. At first Michael couldn't tell whether they were effective. But after the first month or so, Michael felt great relief. His therapist warned him from increasing the dose. Sometimes, Michael would have no choice but to take two, or even three pills. And nowadays, Michael couldn't sleep unless he has his two pills before going to bed.

· · ·

"AAAAAHH!" snapped Michael.

"Michael! Are you alright?"

"Oh, Lucas. It's just another nightmare…" Michael sighed while wiping his face with the blanket. These nightmares became part of his sleep cycle. At first, Lucas would panic; but now even he knew that there was no escaping these reoccurring 'dreams'.

"It's almost four, try to rest, we have a big day tomorrow," Lucas noted, pulling his blanket back up to cover his face.

"Sorry for waking you up…" Michael apologized as he attempted to close his eyes again. "What's the point? The moment I sleep, I will have that same nightmare," he thought, rightfully so. No matter the amount of times Michael had convinced himself that he didn't kill Anna, a voice inside him kept blaming him.

Michael kept on rolling in the bed until the birds started to sing their morning songs outside the window. After losing hope in resting, he hopped off bed to take a cold shower. Lucas dressed up and they were ready to start the new semester; probably just Lucas, for Michael was still suffering from his severe sleep deprivation. The last time he had had a good night sleep was when he slept on Anna's side of the bed; her scent helped relax his mind and kept that voice at bay.

The two arrived early, and Michael suggested eating breakfast. "You know," Lucas spoke, "I miss my life back home. I had my friends and was almost living the dream. It was until Rita offered me to spy on Anna. Everything changed since then. I'm not sure it was worth my time."

Michael continued to eat his omelet as he listened to Lucas' past life. "You still have time to create a brighter future. At least you have a lovely family," he added.

"I guess you are right. I made a promise to my parents, I told them that I'll return back home with a degree that they can be proud of. As the only son, I think this is the least I can do," explained Lucas.

"All right, I think it's time to go. My class starts in ten minutes," remarked Michael.

"I'll stay here, I have some time left."

Michael arrived at the class; a small room with about forty something chairs. He walked around to find the perfect location, then sat down and placed his bag near him. Shortly afterwards, students started to enter the class; one after another, boys, and girls. The door was opened; Michael turned his head to take a look, "A girl?" he thought. Michael fixed his eyes on her, as she sat down ahead of him. Her seat was north-west to where he was facing. The professor entered the class moments later.

"Good morning, ladies and gentlemen," she spoke in an audible manner.

"Good morning," replied the students; except Michael, who was still gazing at that uncanny girl. He was almost certain that he'd never seen her before here at UAM.

"She has white hair, with some black here and there. She is whiter than the rest, nothing about her seems normal. But what is this that I'm feeling? I feel a rather bizarre feeling towards her. Is this some sort of butterfly effect?" Michael wondered as he drifted away from reality.

"My name is Sophia, and I will be your Communication course professor," said Sophia. She then proceeded to take the attendance. Michael regained his focus and waited for his name; which was number 20, he thus had to listen to all those before his name.

"Claire," called Sophia.

"Here!"

Michael flicked his eyes to that girl, "Claire, huh..." He thought.

"Michael," called Sophia.

"Yes, here," snapped Michael.

After taking the attendance, Sophia started with an introductory presentation; nothing special, at least for Michael.

Michael had a one-hour break before his next class. He returned back to the same cafe hoping to find the white girl who had captured his mind and possible soul... There, Michael sat in the same place and grabbed a book out of his bag. While reading, Michael took his eyes off his book and saw Claire sitting at a nearby table; his heart pounded as he tried to avoid eye contact.

# APPROACH

T<sub>HE</sub> FOLLOWING MORNING, M<sub>ICHAEL</sub> WOKE UP FEELING refreshed; those nightmares didn't bother him last night. He sat on the bed's edge and thought about what he had encountered yesterday.

"Michael, wanna grab breakfast?" asked Lucas. Michael nodded; his mind was already preoccupied processing.

"Good morning," beamed the barista behind the counter.

"I'll have black coffee please," said Lucas.

"What about you?" asked the barista. "Um, I'll have this," Michael grabbed one of the displayed sandwiches.

Michael sat down in a quiet manner, which was unlike him; Lucas attempted to comprehend what was going on, but he couldn't read Michael's poker face. "What's wrong?" he finally asked.

"It's nothing—"

"Are you sure?" insisted Lucas.

"Fine, I'll tell you," sighed Michael. "Yesterday, I met this strange girl. Her name is Claire, and I'm sure I never met her before," explained Michael.

"So?"

"Whenever I see her, my chest hurts. It's a strange feeling that I've never experienced before," added Michael.

"This feeling you're experiencing is called love!" chuckled Lucas, then continued, "didn't you love Anna? You must have felt the same before."

Michael shook his head, "What I had with Anna was different. I didn't see her as a lover, but rather a companion. Sure, my feelings for her changed later on, but I can't recall having this sort of pain…"

Michael ate in a hurry, and then ran ahead of Lucas. His class starts in thirty minutes; using the metro, he could barely make it in time. Michael sat in his usual spot by the window. He loved looking outside the window; seeing people running to work, and cars struggling through the traffic. The train halted; new people hopped in, while some exited. Michael turned to scan his surrounding environment, trying to observe the different faces. Something grabbed his attention, "Claire! What was she doing here?" he wondered. Claire looked his way and smiled; Michael quickly flicked his eyes to the window on his right.

After arriving, Michael stepped out of the metro. He waited for Claire to exit, but she remained seated in her place. The metro's doors slid close, and it started to move.

"I bet she doesn't have any classes today, lucky her..." he thought in an attempt to suppress the otherwise bugging thoughts he had. Michael walked to his class; it was empty, as usual. He sat and reached for a notebook from his bag.

"Good morning! You must be Michael. I'm from student affairs, can you come with me for a while?"

"Um, sure," said Michael. He packed his stuff and walked behind the man.

They arrived at the student affairs room. It was filled

with office cubicles divided by some sort of partition. "Please, have a seat," said the lady sitting in the office chair.

"We brought you today to talk about your academic success. The past two semesters were outstanding; you managed to score a GPA of 3.8! As a result for this achievement, we would like to invite you to attend a small ceremony. It's a yearly event that only those who have scored more than 3.5 points can attend," explained the lady.

"I'd be honored to attend this ceremony. When exactly will it be held?" Michael asked.

"This Friday, at seven in the evening. I'll email you the location later today."

"Oh, by the way, parents are more than welcomed to join you on this special night."

"My dad is dead, and my mom is blind. She lives in Los Angeles."

"Sorry to hear that…"

Michael returned back to his class. He wasn't that interested in the ceremony, but he certainly was proud of his work. The class was packed, and the professor began taking the attendance. "What's your name?" he asked.

"Michael, Michael Walker."

"All right, Michael, have a seat." All the seats were taken, except for one in the front row. Michael had no choice but to sit there.

"My name is Isaac, and welcome to Calculus Two."

"Are you sure it's all right for me to come?" inquired the now excited Lucas.

"Yeah, I get to bring two guests," noted Michael while fixing his grey tie.

"Fine, if you say so," sighed Lucas, a desperate attempt to hide his utter joy.

"I'll go find a cab. Get dressed and meet me outside," remarked Michael.

Michael waved his hands at a parked taxi, the driver opened the window, "Where you going?" he asked.

"I'm going there," Michael pointed at the map in his phone.

"All right, get in."

Lucas came running to the car. "We're ready," remarked Michael.

It was a ten minute drive to the ceremony location. Lucas and Michael paid the driver and strolled toward the entrance.

"Names," said the security guard by the front door.

"Michael."

"Michael Larry Walker?"

"Yup, and this is my guest," replied Michael.

"Ladies and Gentlemen, I would like to congratulate you on your academic success," said Vince.

"Now, we shall call names starting from the highest GPA," he continued.

Michael was preparing to stand up when Vince called the first name, "Claire Wyatt."

"What!" snapped Michael.

"What's wrong?" asked Lucas.

"That's the girl I told you about."

"Michael Walker," called Vince.

Michael stood up and walked to the stage. He shook hands with Vince and received his certificate. Michael then had to stand next to Claire as Vince called the rest. His heart was pounding; Michael tried to calm himself down. "Congratulations!" He whispered.

"Thanks," smiled Claire.

Finally, all students were on stage forming three rows. After taking a group photo, the students scattered all over the stage. Proud parents started to clap as each student returned to his parents; except Michael, he had Lucas waiting by his seat.

A little buffet was available for guests. "I haven't eaten lunch yet. Come on, let's eat!" said Lucas.

"No, I already had lunch," replied Michael as he was eyeing the lonely Claire sitting by herself. Apparently, Claire didn't bring any guest with her. Michael felt this was the perfect opportunity to approach her.

"Aren't you going to eat?" asked Michael as he stood to her right.

"I don't feel like it," Claire replied showing a disappointed face.

"Is everything alright?"

"No," Claire said, "life isn't going so well."

"Why? What's wrong?"

"I'm sure you've already noticed that I'm different from everybody else. My hair is white, my skin is pale—nothing about me screams normal," explained Claire. "I thought if I proved to people that I was just like them; they might accept me... I was wrong. No matter how hard I tried to impress them, they just kept on rejecting me," she added.

Michael saw the sorrowfulness in her face; he had no idea what to say, and how to act in response. "I-I don't think you are different," he hesitated.

"You really think so?"

"People have no right to judge you by your looks. If so, you're the most beautiful woman I've ever seen."

"What am I saying!" Michael thought to himself, as his blushed ever so slightly.

"No one ever said such things to me, this makes me happy," smiled Claire.

"Michael, I'm returning, you wanna come along?" yelled Lucas from across the hall.

"I'm coming—"

"Wait!" Claire grabbed Michael's arm.

"Um, thanks for your kind words."

Michael smiled, then rushed to Lucas.

"What were you two talking about?" grinned Lucas.

"Nothing special, I was just congratulating her for being the top student," explained Michael.

Upon arriving, Lucas went to take a shower; while Michael covered his face with the now cool blanket. "I can't believe what I just told Claire. That was very impulsive of me… I hope she doesn't get the wrong idea about me," he then took his two pills and switched off the lamp near his bed.

"MORNING," greeted Sophia as she walked by the door. "Before we start, how about we play a small game. The rules are simple, each one has to say three statements about themselves—two are true, and one is a lie. Your job is to identify which one is the lie."

Students began to take turns; and their colleagues took guesses, some were right, others were wrong. Finally, it was Michael's turn. "I've never been to New York. I've been engaged but never married. I have a twin," Michael said whatever came to his mind at that precise moment.

"The engagement one is a lie," said a guy sitting behind Michael.

Michael shook his head.

After several random guesses, Claire raised her hands.

"You have a twin; that was a lie." Michael nodded. The students were chattering, Arabic, Indian, and English; each group with their mother tongue.

"Moving on, we have… Claire," read Sophia off the paper she held.

Claire stood up, and Michael turned his seat to have a better look at her. "Um, let's see…" she hesitated, "I know how to play the piano, I'm afraid of blood, and I hate traveling."

No one answered; Michael knew that they were trying to contempt her. "The third statement was a lie," he said. Claire nodded and sat down quickly. She was already embarrassed by the student; although Michael's answer was wrong, Claire wanted to get over with this thing.

"Now that we broke the ice, let's start with our main goal for this class," began Sophia.

The class went by smoothly; and before dismissing it, Sophia asked the students to form groups of three students. These groups will be used for assignments and projects. Each three gathered and wrote their names. "Anyone who hasn't found a group, please stand up," remarked Sophia. Three students stood up: Michael, Claire, and Lyla. "Great, you three will be together," she said.

The three students looked at each other; Lyla was afraid of working with Claire, after all the rumors she had heard. Lyla thus nervously smiled at Claire before taking a seat.

After the students have left, Michael walked to Lyla. "Hey, can I have your number? We have to create a messaging group," Michael said.

"Um, sure…" Lyla hesitated.

Michael then rushed to catch on Claire, who was about to leave the class. "Claire, may I have your phone number."

"Of course!" she smiled.

"Thanks," said Michael as he handed the phone.

"U-um... if you're free tonight, I need help with my calculus homework," hesitated Claire.

"Sure," Michael answered at once.

"I know a great cafe near the Emirates Towers station. Let's say around seven, how's that?" she suggested.

"Sounds great, I'll see you then," smiled Michael.

Lucas was waiting for Michael near the main entrance; Michael promised to eat lunch with him. "What took you so long?"

"We had to create groups, and I wasn't selected in any. Basically, my group was the only group with three members; me, Claire, and a third girl," explained Michael.

"I see, at least now you can be close to that Claire," teased Lucas.

"Don't get the wrong idea, we were the only students with no groups," remarked Michael. "So, where do you wanna eat?"

"Remember that restaurant near your old hotel?"

"All right, if you say so," sighed Michael.

"Oh right... Anna had her stroke there. I'm sorry, let's choose somewhere else."

"No, it's all right." Michael wanted to get over Anna's death; he desperately wanted to convince himself that he didn't kill her. By going to that restaurant, Michael was hoping he could get over his past.

"Hey, it's you again! Sorry about your girlfriend," said the waiter.

"Hi, we want a table for two please."

"Got it, right this way."

Flashbacks appeared in Michael's mind; after all, Anna had a stroke right in this very place. "Anna..." Michael muttered.

Lucas realized this table was where Anna had her unfortunate accident. "Um, can we change tables? How about that one over there?" The waiter nodded. Michael tried to clear his mind; he could still see Anna fainting at that table. He tried to shake his head, but that didn't work either.

"Michael, you all right?"

"I'm fine…" assured Michael.

Michael ate lunch, then went back home to prepare for the night.

# CHANCE

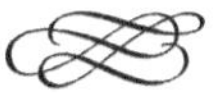

"A NNA... W AIT... D ON'T GO!" MUMBLED M ICHAEL.

"Michael! Michael, wake up. You are having a nightmare," Lucas tried to shake Michael's trembling body. He woke up at last; his face pale and visibly distorted, "It wasn't a nightmare. I saw Anna!" he rejoiced while catching his fleeting breath.

"What?"

"Anna's spirit… she came to me," explained Michael.

"How can you be certain it wasn't just a dream?" inquired Lucas.

"I don't know. All I know is that she was the Anna I've always known."

"What did she come for?" asked Lucas.

"You woke me before hearing what she wanted." Remarked Michael, "Anyway, I'm going to meet Claire."

"A date!"

"No. She wanted my help with this math assignment," explained Michael.

"It always starts like this. Next thing you know, you're on a date with her," remarked Lucas.

Michael dressed up and walked to the metro station. He arrived at the café and began looking around for a girl with white hair. "She's not here yet..."

Claire walked to the table shortly afterwards, "Sorry, I lost track of time!"

"It's alright."

"These are the questions," Claire handed her notebook.

After twenty minutes of tutoring, Claire managed to wrap up her homework assignment. "Thanks for your help, really appreciate it."

"No problem, glad I could help. If you need anything, please let me know," smiled Michael.

Both stared at each other for a solid minute, before Claire stood up, "I gotta go; see you in class." Michael waved at her as she left the cafe strolling, having ridden herself off the rather hefty assessment for the evening.


A WEEK LATER, Michael was getting ready for his first group project. The group had to collect information from the public library. Michael knew it was going to be tough dealing with two introverted girls. "All right, each one will search alone, we will then discuss the findings."

"Sounds good," said Claire. Lyla simply nodded.

"So, Lyla, are you from here?" Claire asked.

"Actually, I'm from Kuwait," answered Lyla.

"Kuwait, huh..."

After thirty minutes or so, the three were gathered at the promised spot. "Found anything interesting?" asked Michael. Claire and Lyla handed over their notes, and he flipped through them, then sat them aside.

"All right, that'll do just fine!" he remarked. Lyla was quick to leave, while Claire stayed as she was. Michael was sorting the papers and Claire kept staring at him.

"So, are you free tonight? I heard they are premiering that horror movie," she at last initiated the conversation.

"I don't see why not. But let me check with my room-mate," remarked Michael.

"You mean that blonde guy you always hang out with?"

"You know him?"

"Nah, I just observe."

"Hey, you have my number, check with him then give me a call, will ya?"

"Sure!" beamed Michael as he packed his stuff.

It was five and the sun was near setting; Lucas has just arrived home. He saw Michael laying on the coach, while covering his eyes with his right hand. "What's going on?" inquired Lucas.

"Oh, you're back. Hey listen, Claire asked me to go with her tonight," explained Michael.

"And?"

"I'm nervous, I don't know what to do… Should I accept her invitation? Or give a generic excuse?"

"Where are you going?" inquired Lucas.

"Some sort of horror movie."

"Wow… Wouldn't call it a date though," shrugged Lucas. "Why are you nervous about it? A girl wants to hang out with you."

"That's the problem, she's a girl! I told you I'm over rela-tionships, especially after what happened last time I thought I was in love…" Lucas sat down, right next to him. He took off his shoes and aligned them near Michael's.

"Hey, I got an idea," snapped Lucas, "Why don't I tag along? This way, you'll be less nervous."

"You? I don't know…" Michael hesitated.

"Come on! It's going to be alright. Plus, I have nothing to do," insisted Lucas.

"Fine…" sighed Michael; he then dialed Claire's number,

before walking out of the apartment to have some privacy. "Hi, it's me, Michael."

"Oh hey Michael... So, have you decided yet?"

"Yup, I'll see you tonight! By the way, when does the movie start?" asked Michael.

"Um, I think nine thirty."

"Great! I'll meet you near the ticket counter."

"Alright, bye!" Claire hung up the call; and Michael returned to Lucas.

"So?"

"The movie starts around nine thirty. We have to be there at least thirty minutes in advance."

"We still have like four hours, I want to take a quick nap," noted Lucas. Michael nodded; as he reached for a book from within his backpack and began reading on the coach.

"WE'RE HERE; where is that Claire?"

"I bet she's on her way. I mean we kinda arrived earlier than usual," remarked Michael.

After standing for seven minutes or so, Michael started looking around at random. He finally found a white-haired woman walking towards them. "There she comes..."

"Hey, Michael. Are you ready?" smiled Claire?

"Sur—"

"Hi, my name is Lucas. I'm Michael's roommate," Lucas interrupted with a huge smile up his innocent face. Meanwhile, Claire's expression changed; as she tried to stay calm and show a smile of her own.

"Um, nice to meet you," she said.

"Sorry, I had to bring him. I hope you have no problem," apologized Michael.

"No... not at all..." smiled Claire.

The three bought tickets and waited as people gathered around the entrance. Shortly afterwards, the doors were opened. "Sorry, I gotta go to the toilet. Can you reserve my seat?" spoke Claire.

"Sure," replied Michael.

Michael and Lucas sat down together. After Claire returned, she was forced to sit next to Lucas; despite her failed attempts to make it obvious for Michael that they should sit together as a couple, Michael was talking with Lucas and didn't realize that Claire was pissed off. "Damn you Lucas; trying to interrupt my chances with Michael," she thought. Claire eventually gave up and settled in her seat near Lucas.

After ten minutes, the lights were dimmed, and the ads stopped; the movie finally started. Claire stared at Michael one last time before shifting her attention to the movie.

"Hey, you want a drink?" whispered Claire to the neighboring Lucas. "Um, sure!" he whispered back enthusiastically. Claire smiled as she handed him the drink.

"And now I wait…" she thought.

The movie concluded after some ninety minutes, and the lights were back on. "How was the movie?" asked Claire.

"Not that bad, if I may say so. I also loved the ending," answered Michael.

"What about you Lucas?" asked Michael; Lucas didn't respond.

"What's wrong?" inquired Claire.

"Sorry… I have to head… head back." He struggled.

"Why?" questioned Michael as he tapped on Lucas's shoulders. "I- I don't know what's going on, my stomach hurts so badly," hesitated Lucas.

"Alright, do you want me to help you on the way back?" offered Michael.

"No… I'll be fine. You guys have fun…" Lucas waddled his way to the exit.

"Sorry about your roommate," apologized Claire, not meaning a single word she had uttered.

"It's alright."

"Say, wanna grab dinner? I know a great restaurant by that dancing fountain."

"I guess so," shrugged Michael, a bit worried about his struggling friend.

It was almost midnight; and Michael felt a tad sleepy, but tried to keep up with the still very energized Claire. "She seems fully awaken," he thought.

"So, Michael, I heard you got engaged but never married. How was it?"

"It's a long story… long and complicated," responded Michael with a sigh.

"We have time," smiled Claire "it's not like you have anything else do now. Am I right?"

"Should I tell her? I'm not sure I can trust her," Michael thought.

"So? Are you gonna tell me or what?" For a split of a second, Michael saw Anna in Claire's face.

"Anna," he muttered.

"I used to live in a wealthy family. They controlled every aspect of my life. I tried to live with it until that night… They told me I have to marry a girl I never met! She was older than me and wasn't even interested in me. At that moment I realized it was time to cut loose," Michael paused and looked at Claire; she appeared to be enjoying the story so far. "I escaped the night of the wedding. And here I am, living in Dubai."

"What about that 'Anna' you just mumbled?" inquired Claire.

"Oh, she also escaped with me. Too bad she didn't live that long afterwards…"

"Why? What happened?"

"She had a stroke—" Michael paused.

"I'm sorry to hear that."

Michael stood up, "Sorry, I have to head back…" He placed his share of the bill on the table and walked out.

"Anna you say? This should be interesting…" muttered Claire showing a strange grin.

Michael hurried back to Lucas; the lights were out and the door left slightly opened.

"Hey, how are you now?" Lucas was already asleep. Michael changed his clothes and went straight to bed.

"WHAT HAPPENED TO YOU LAST NIGHT?" asked Michael.

"I'm not sure. All I know is that I spent the rest of the evening in the bathroom," explained Lucas.

"Feel any better now?"

"I guess so. The pain was gone after I demolished that toilet…" Michael tried to recall what Lucas ate yesterday. Everything he ate, Michael, too, ate from.

"Anyway, I have a calculus quiz. Will you be alright on your own?" asked Michael.

"Don't worry about me, I won't take the day off," remarked Lucas.

Michael hurried to the metro station. There, he grabbed a sandwich from a small booth, and then went up to the platform.

He took his time as he strolled around campus; he still had twenty minutes before the quiz started. A cool breeze started blowing; Michael had to rush to the class with five minutes remaining.

"All right, the quiz will last an hour. After you finish, feel free to leave," instructed Isaac. The students flipped the quiz paper; some were shocked, others were relieved. Michael had nothing to be worried about. He grabbed his pen and commenced solving.

"Thirty minutes left," remarked Isaac. Michael wrote his name then handed over his quiz paper. "Already done?"

"Yup."

"You still have time to revise."

"It's alright, I came here prepared," smiled Michael. Isaac smiled back and took the paper. Michael recalled his old days at school; he would wrap up the test while the rest were still struggling at the third question.

"Oh, Michael!" called Sophia. Michael turned his head, "Hi, Professor."

"I read your first project deliverable. I gotta say, I'm impressed."

"Thanks, I'm glad you enjoyed it."

"By the way, the second deliverable is right around the corner. It's due next Tuesday if I'm not mistaken. You have to meet with your group and get an early start," remarked Sophia.

"And what exactly do we have to do?" inquired Michael.

"You're going to shoot a video. It'll include all your findings from the first deliverable," explained Sophia.

"Got it." replied Michael.

MICHAEL SAT IN THE CAFE; his second class was after thirty minutes. "I just talked with Sophia. She loved our first project; also, she explained the second part of the project. We have to shoot a video explaining our findings. Anyone has a place in mind?" texted Michael.

"Sorry, I live with my grandparents," replied Lyla.

"It's all right," he texted back.

"Me too, I live in a small apartment. What about you, Michael?" texted Claire.

"I guess we can meet in my apartment. How about tomorrow evening? My roommate has a class, so we will have the whole place to ourselves."

"Sure!" replied Claire.

"I have no problem," replied Lyla.

"Great, I'll send over the location."

# MEETING

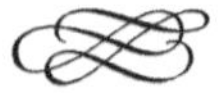

Michael quickly cleaned the apartment. He made the beds and cleared the table. Lucas had left for his class, and Michael was waiting for his group to arrive. The phone vibrated; it was a text. "I just got off the metro, give me five minutes max," texted Claire. Michael changed his clothes and waited for the door knock.

"Hello?" called Claire from outside the door. Michael rushed to open the door.

"Hi! Sorry for being late."

"N- No problem," Michael gazed upon Claire. She had a black shirt with average-looking jeans. He shook his head and welcomed her inside.

"So, this is where you live, huh? not bad."

"Have a seat," offered Michael. "Wanna drink something?"

"No, I'm good," replied Claire.

Shortly afterwards, Lyla knocked the door. "It was my first time riding the metro. Took me a while to realize where I was heading," explained Lyla.

"I see... Now shall we start?" Michael sat a tripod with the camera fixed on top. Each member took a turn in talking about their part of the project.

As Michael was shooting his part, the front door was opened. "Hey Mich—Whoa, what's going on here?"

"Lucas… Forgot to tell you, but we kinda have a group meeting here," explained Michael.

Lucas was silent, his eyes caught Lyla working with the camera. "Um, hi, my name is Lucas. Nice to meet you," he approached her at once.

"Hi, I'm Lyla, the pleasure is mine."

Michael and Claire waited for Lucas to return back to reality. "Ahem, sorry for interrupting your meeting. I'll be in the next room," said Lucas; his eyes were fixed on Lyla as he strolled towards the neighboring bedroom.

"What was that about?" Michael thought, then resumed the recording as to catch up with the fleeing time.

"THAT WAS THE LAST PART; now I just have to edit the video, and it will be ready for submission!"

"Great! Now if you don't mind, I have a metro to deal with," chuckled Lyla.

"Sure, see you tomorrow."

"I should probably return back too. Thanks for every-thing, Michael."

Michael showed a thumbs up sign, along a smile he was still getting used to.

"Lucas, they're gone. No need to hide!" he then called.

"What's the deal with that girl? Who is she?" asked Lucas.

"Oh, Lyla? What about her? Don't tell me... You fell for her!"

"I don't know... The way she glanced back at me... I might be in love!"

"You know she's from Kuwait?"

"So what? It doesn't matter where did she came from. Love is a universal language!"

"Um, can I have her number? You have it, right?"

"Fine, but don't blame me if she rejects you," sighed Michael.

"I have nothing to lose!" laughed Lucas.

Michael sat down on the beds edge and placed the laptop on his lap.

"Hey, can I turn off the lights? I haven't gotten any sleep lately," asked Lucas.

"Sure," replied Michael.

"Have you heard?" added Lucas as he was getting comfortable in bed.

"About what?"

"The field trip. Apparently we'll be going on a trip to London!"

"What, no one told me about any trip," Michael closed the laptop.

"Strange, perhaps they're still spreading the word."

"London, huh... Sure, why not!" thought Michael while pushing through a smile.

THE CLASS WAS DISMISSED, and Michael remained in his seat to pack his stuff. He observed as students walked out of the door; they were then followed by Sophia, then Lyla. Michael scanned the classroom and realized that he was once again alone with Claire. "I gotta walk out before this gets awkward," thought Michael as he immediately zipped his backpack.

"Um, Michael," called Claire from the other side of the class. Michael turned his head to face her, "Yeah?"

"So, are you going to the trip?" she inquired.

"I don't know. What about you?"

"Of course, I love London!"

"I see," Said Michael, "I just can't see the purpose behind the trip."

"It doesn't need a purpose, at least we'll escape this heat."

"I'll think about it," Michael pushed open the door, aiming for the library; for he had to study for his psychology assignment. He wasn't intending on taking psychology just because it reminded him of Lisa. But then he realized that it could be an 'easy A', and his mother was no longer a weighing factor.

"Michael," Lucas tapped on Michael's back.

"Oh hey Lucas…" whispered back Michael.

"So, have you decided?" he pulled a chair and sat next to Michael.

Michael knew that he couldn't study with Lucas hanging around. "I'm still thinking about it," he replied while packing his notebook.

"You only have until tomorrow to decide. I heard the university doesn't want a packed plane. That's why no one told you in person," explained Lucas. Michael tried giving it a quick thought.

"Alright, were can I register?" he finally spoke.

"Come with me, I was on my way when I passed by you." Michael had thirty minutes or so to spare. They walked for a while before reaching an office. At the entrance, a small sign was hanging. 'Register for the field trip' was printed on said sign. Lucas knocked the door and entered immediately.

"Hi, we would like to apply for the trip."

"Absolutely! Here, fill these papers. You have until tomorrow 5PM to bring them back." The guy handed them each two papers.

"So, when is the trip anyway?" questioned Michael.

"I think in two weeks. Eighth of October, to be more accurate."

"What about the midterms?"

"The midterms are in November," noted Lucas "we'll be back long before!"

"All right, I have a group assignment, see you back home," noted Michael. Lucas nodded as Michael was picking up the pace to his class.

"Is that Lyla?" wondered Lucas. He walked slowly behind her. Lyla noticed someone was following her; she turned her head to find Lucas sneaking behind her. "Oh, hi. Lyla? Am I saying it correctly?" he hesitated.

"And you are… Lucas?"

"Yup! So, how was the project?" asked Lucas.

"It went by smoothly, thanks to Michael," acknowledged Lyla.

"Excellent! Did you hear about the upcoming trip?"

"You mean London? Yeah, I already applied."

"Great, I just took the papers." Lyla glanced at her watch once again; Lucas realized she was in a hurry. "I have to go, see you soon," he hurried the other direction.

"See you soon," replied Lyla.

"I think she likes me!"

It was the night before the trip. Michael and Lucas were making some final checking. "Can't wait for tomorrow!" rejoiced Lucas.

"Me too!"

"By the way, how's things going on between you and Lyla?" asked Michael.

"Well, the first dinner was great. But I'm not familiar with her culture. Not sure if they take things slow or fast," explained Lucas.

"Actually, there are no 'things' to start with," remarked Michael.

"What do you mean?"

"People in this area aren't that open about 'love at first sight' concept. They prefer someone from their society."

"Wait, are you saying that I have no chance with Lyla?"

"I'm not saying that. Obviously some are open-minded. I guess you have to take your chances," explained Michael.

After closing the bags, Michael placed his clothes on the couch. He then took his shiny blue pill before going to bed.

THE NEXT MORNING, Lucas woke up around six; he found Michael standing by the window. "Since when were you up?"

"Since two thirty," Michael replied, "I saw her!"

"Who?"

"Anna! She came to me last night."

"Really!"

"Yeah, although something strange happened," noted Michael. "I was talking with her, when suddenly it got dark; like really dark. I called for her but got no response. After walking around, I saw a white-haired beast eating something. I wanted to see what he was chowing on, but the moment that beast looked my way, I woke up."

"Wow," said Lucas; as he had nothing else to say.

"It's almost time, dress up." Michael nodded, as he gaze at the birds through the window.

Both arrived at the airport; they were the first to arrive. "When were we supposed to meet?"

"Around seven thirty," replied Lucas.

Michael checked his phone's clock, "It's seven fifteen…"

"I think someone's coming our way," noted Lucas.

"Her name is Sophia."

"Oh Michael! Are you ready?" asked Sophia showing her usual beaming smile.

"Yeah." answered Michael with a less enthusiastic tone.

"Hi, I'm Lucas, Michael's friend."

"Oh, nice to meet you Lucas."

The group grew larger and wider. And after thirty minutes, all students were finally together. The university had assigned three instructors to watch over the twelve students participating in the trip. From the twenty five students that applied, only twelve were able to confirm their participation. "Everyone, gather here please," called Sophia. "I want each two students to form a pair together," she added.

Students searched for their pairs; the group ended up with six pairs. Michael was debating between Lucas and Claire; but Lucas was after Lyla from the start. Michael saw Claire waving at him and paired with her. "Great! Now we have around 45 minutes before the departure. Each pair can walk around, but make sure you return 20 minutes before departure," remarked Sophia. Each pair took off; they have a whole terminal to explore and get lost in.

"Aren't you gonna walk around?" asked Claire.

"I just want a cup of coffee. If it's all right with you, I want to sit at a cafe or something."

"No problem!" approved Claire.

Lucas and Lyla walked around and ended up eating at a fancy restaurant. It was Lucas' intentions to show Lyla that he is capable of eating in such fancy places.

It was 8:15AM when students began lining up to enter the plane. After everyone was settled in their seats, flight attendants walked by to make last minutes check. Claire stared at Michael as he closed his eyes for a nap; meanwhile Lucas and Lyla sat in the row right behind them. The flight was ready to depart.

# CONFESS

"A-Anna…" muttered Michael.

"ANNA!" He shrieked moments later.

"Hey, you alright?" inquired Claire.

Lucas tapped on Michael's back from his seat, "Buddy, take your pills."

"Thanks," Michael said as he picked the pill from Lucas' hand. Michael had attempted to go back to Anna, who was apparently waiting in his dream.

"Sir, we're about to land. Please return your seat to its original position," said the lady walking by. Michael fixed his seat; he then picked a magazine stashed behind the seat in front of him.

"Can I ask a question?" Claire leaned to Michael's seat.

"Sure."

"So, this Anna… does she mean anything to you?"

"It's complicated…" remarked Michael.

"Is that so?"

"At first, I didn't really think of her as a 'girl'; but rather a tool to help me reach my goal. Later on, I realized she was more than a 'tool'; perhaps, a 'companion'. Too bad she died before I could express my feelings." added Michael.

The plane landed and strolled around, trying to find the gate in which to stop at. The whole landing process took around thirty minutes. And after the seatbelt sign was turned off, Michael packed his stuff and waited eagerly for his partner Claire. "Here we are, London!" thought Michael as he was walking towards the arrival hall.

Pairs took turns to grab their luggage from the moving belt. Then, students were assembled near the exit. "In a few minutes, a bus will arrive to pick us. We will go to the hotel; there, each pair will settle in their room," announced Sophia.

The bus arrived and pairs hopped on; one after another. "Michael, over here!" waved Lucas. Lucas had reserved the last row for Michael and his partner. The four settled in back there; with Michael sitting by the window, followed by Claire, Lyle, and Lucas, who was sitting on the other end of the row.

The students checked in their rooms; each two rooms were separated by a door. Michael asked Sophia if she could give Lucas the room near his. "The professor said today is a free day. Any suggestions?" inquired Lyla.

"Well, it's more like a free night," chuckled Lucas, "the sun sat down the moment we landed!"

"I guess we could go for a walk, if that's all right with you," he added.

"Yeah, sure; I mean it's still five."

"Hey, Michael, wanna go walk around?" asked Lucas as he knocked the door.

"Sorry, I got other plans," replied Michael from the other side of the door.

"I guess it's just you and me!" rejoiced Lucas.

The two walked to a nearby bridge. Along the bridge

were blue lights that lighten up the path to the other side of it. People walking both directions as a couple, or simply a lonely man. "Pretty, isn't it?" said Lucas; Lyla nodded as she was enjoying the lights. Lucas stood next to her, who was leaning against the bridge, gazing upon River Thames.

"Look at those cruise ships roaming around everywhere. Their blue lights are reflecting on the river surface…I-I can't express this feeling!"

"You wanna go join them?" asked Lucas.

"Oh no, I have sea sickness," explained Lyla.

The night wind became more furious. Lucas was enjoying the sight when he heard Lyla's chattering teeth. "Here," he handed over his coat.

"Are you sure? You might get a cold."

"It's all right, I'm used to this breeze," smiled Lucas.

"Thanks," whispered Lyla as she wore the coat.

"So, wanna go find something to eat?" suggested Lucas.

"Yeah, I'm starving!"

The two walked across the bridge; there, Lucas eyed an Italian restaurant. "Buonasera," said the waiter.

"Hi, a table for two please," replied Lucas. The waiter nodded and walked ahead. Lucas locked his eyes on Lyla as she sat down. Lyla then looked back at Lucas; both kept their eyes engaged for a moment or so.

Lucas tried to break this awkward silence, "So, have you decided on what to eat?"

"Um, no…you?" Lucas shook his head then grabbed the menu placed in front of him.

"Ready to order?" inquired a waitress passing by.

"I'll have this," pointed Lucas.

"And you madam?"

"Um… I'll have what he is having," spoke Lyla. The waitress nodded as she wrote down the order on a small tablet. It was the same silence all over again. Lucas had no idea how to behave in front of a Middle Eastern girl. He didn't want to do anything that might be considered as 'rude' by Lyla's culture.

"Um—"

"Lucas, I have something to tell you," interrupted Lyla.

"What is it?"

"I know this might sound a bit crazy; and I don't know how you guys do stuff back in America. But I think I have feelings for you," Lyla hesitated as she spoke.

Lucas' heart pounded; blood was rushing all through his then shivering body. His face turned bright red, and he had nothing to say. Lucas waited for his heart to slow down a bit.

"Did I mess things up?" inquired Lyla.

"No! It's just that I'm a bit shocked," explained Lucas.

"In the past eighteen years, I've only had one relationship. To make things worse, we broke up, and now she's dead," added Lucas.

"Oh my god! I'm sorry, I didn't know you had such past," apologized Lyla.

"It's all right. To be honest, I'm glad you had a feeling for me. I was starting to believe that I'll die alone. I have no friends. Well, except for Michael. Also, I'm not that good with women," remarked Lucas.

"Why would you say such things? That's not true! I love you, and I'm a girl!" smiled Lyla.

Lucas couldn't control himself; tears slipped out of his eyes. "I'm sorry, I guess I became more emotional over time," he smiled.

"Sir, madam," called the waitress as she approached their table. "Enjoy your dinner…"

Lucas ate while still gazing at Lyla. He still couldn't process that Lyla has feelings for him. Just when he thought love was a myth, Lyla became the light he reached for.

After dinner, it was still seven; Lucas thought it was still early to head back. "Where do you wanna go now?" he inquired.

"I'm not sure... I mean it's my first time here." replied Lyla.

"How about a movie?" suggested Lucas.

"Sure!"

"Then it's settled, I'll look for the nearest movie theater."

MICHAEL AND CLAIRE were in their room. The two stayed behind to relax after the seven-hour flight. "Ready to go?" inquired Michael.

"What time is it?" asked Claire as she was stretching up.

"It's seven thirty," answered Michael.

"Where you wanna go anyway?"

"I thought we could go for a walk," explained Michael.

"Sure, just give me a sec to dress up," winked Claire as she walked to the bathroom.

"I'll wait outside by the entrance."

"Whoa! It's cold out here," thought Michael, as he rubbed his hands together just to keep them warm. Shortly afterwards, Michael saw Claire walking out of the elevator.

"Sorry for keeping you waiting," said Claire.

"I-it's all right," replied Michael as he fixed his eyes on her white hair, getting blown by the breeze.

Michael and Claire walked randomly for twenty minutes. They had no specific destination in mind; well, at least Claire didn't. "You know... While waiting for you, I looked online for some spots. I found a great park that's not far away," remarked Michael.

"Great! Let's check it out," approved Claire.

"I forgot to ask, but aren't you cold? You're wearing a long sleeve shirt, and that's it! No jacket, no scarf, just the shirt."

"It's alright, at this point, I can't really feel the cold on my skin," explained Claire with a serious tone.

"What?" Michael showed a puzzled face; he tried to analyze her statement but failed.

"Just kidding," laughed Claire; Michael laughed along.

The park was empty, the lake was still, and the animals were asleep. Both walked around the park until they reached a bridge. The bridge connected the two sides of the lake. Michael and Claire walked halfway through the bridge then stopped. Claire leant her back on the handrail, "The moon looks beautiful."

"Yeah..." replied Michael as he leaned next to her.

"Michael..."

"Hmm?"

"Can I ask you something?" Claire faced Michael.

"Sure."

"Why do you keep on hanging out with me disregarding what others say about me?"

"Because I don't think you're weird."

"But how can you know that for sure?"

Michael took a deep breath, then continued, "I feel that we have some sort of connection."

"What do you mean?" Claire moved even closer to Michael.

"You remind me of her..." sighed Michael. "I promised myself after Anna's death that I wouldn't fall in love again. Yet, it's as if I'm seeing her in you!" he added.

"So, you only hang out with me because I remind you of your dead girlfriend?" joked Claire.

"No! I really think you are a great woman. You're smart, beautiful, and... and—" Michael stopped talking. He shifted his eyes to the small lake, "Come to think of it, why did Anna come to me in my dreams?" he wondered. Claire stood silently as Michael was trying to figure out the chaos in his mind.

"Is everything all right?" Claire finally spoke.

"Sorry, I just remembered something," explained Michael.

"Is it about Anna?" asked Claire.

"Kind of... lately, every thought had to be related somehow to Anna," remarked Michael.

"I'll be honest with you, Michael…"

"Ever since that night we first met, I felt something different. I've always isolated myself from society. Not a choice, but rather a reaction."

Michael felt a warm feeling in his heart. He actually did something good for someone. "That night, I only said what I truly felt. My mouth and heart outpaced my brain," smiled Michael.

Claire then stood facing Michael, in which his heart pounded involuntary. Michael could hear Claire's heartbeats; he wanted to back off, but the lake was right behind him. Michael finally gave up to his human urges. No matter how long this fight will last, the body must surrender to the soul. After all, the body is merely the vessel of the soul. Michael saw Claire slowly approaching his lips; he swallowed his wet saliva, then closed his eyes. Within parts of a second, Michael felt a soft thing on his lips.

Suddenly, Anna popped up in Michael's mind. He quickly slipped by Claire to the other side. "What's wrong?" inquired Claire.

"I'm sorry," replied Michael as he was trying to catch his breath.

"I think it's getting late. Maybe we should return," suggested Claire, and Michael nodded.

Back at the hotel, Lucas and Lyla were already in bed

when Michael entered the room. "What took you so long?" asked Lucas from the other room.

"We lost track of time," replied Michael.

Michael brushed his teeth, took his pill, and tucked himself into bed. "Good night, Claire."

"Good night, Michael…" replied Claire with a grin.

# UNVEIL

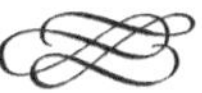

It was 3AM. Claire had wiped her sleepy eyes, before waddling to the bathroom. There, she changed her clothes and splashed some water on her pale face. She picked a bag hidden under her bed; then gently opened the door as to avoid any unwanted attention. "Time to go!" she muttered.

Claire made sure no one was following her as she exited the hotel. She waved at a car waiting near the entrance; a black sedan with tinted windows approached her. "Go, now!" she ordered.

The car drove for fifteen minutes, before stopping near a warehouse. The place was abandoned years ago; smashed glass, broken doors, and secured with a barbed wire. "You wait here."

"I'm here!" said Claire as she entered.

"Claire! Welcome back," rejoiced Scarlett.

"I'm so glad the university arranged this trip. Otherwise, I wouldn't be here eating dinner with you!"

"Have a seat," offered Scarlett. Claire took her seat at the head of the dining table. Scarlett opened a cooler box and grabbed a wrapped plate. She unwrapped it and picked the meat out, placing it on a cutting board. Then, she ignited a portable gas stove. Claire drooled as Scarlett placed the meat on the pan.

"Is it done yet? I can't wait!" Exclaimed Claire from her seat.

"Just a sec," replied Scarlett.

Scarlett took the meat and sliced it into equal portions. "Here you go," she placed the plate in front of Claire, then took the rest for herself.

"Oh, I've been waiting forever for this!" rejoiced Scarlett. "Ever since you disappeared, the process got disturbed. I had to do all the work!"

Claire picked a piece with her fork and gazed at the sauce dripping. "Oh yeah! That's the good stuff!" yelled Claire as she took the first bite. "I can't remember when the last time I ate such tender meat was. How old is she?" Claire couldn't contain her excitement.

"Seventeen, just how we like it. The perfect age. The meat is still tender and easy to slice," replied Scarlett with a mouthful.

"Oh, I almost forgot; I found someone interesting," remarked Claire.

"Someone interesting?"

"The name's Michael. He escaped his wedding and went to Dubai. His life is almost as miserable as mine." Claire explained while wiping her mouth with a napkin.

"Are you planning on introducing him?" inquired Scarlett.

"I'm not sure yet, I wouldn't risk our small 'cult' by such impulsive moves. I need to make sure his spirit is broken—desperate. He has to lose hope in society; the feeling of not belonging anywhere," Claire paused. "The only problem is this 'Anna' he keeps talking about!" she snapped, slamming her knife on the wooden table.

Claire then stood up and walked to the broken window. "Listen, Scarlett, I might not return back for a while."

"What do you mean?"

"I can't risk people seeing me. They will surely remember a white-haired girl walking around after midnight," explained Claire. "Today was an exception; I really craved a girl. Also, when are you planning on moving to Dubai?"

"I know I'm the only girl out of the group that stayed behind. But you know I can't leave my mom alone. Also remember what Trevor told us? It's always better to expand our network," remarked Scarlett.

"I guess you're right. It was all thanks to him we are standing in this place right here!"

"Why are you still with her anyway? Wasn't it enough that she didn't defend you from your crazy father?" snapped Claire, smoothly cruising through her repressed emotions. "It's nice that you got rid of him for your mom's sake. Boy was it some delicious meat!" she added.

"He deserves what he got. Look at all those scars! It was the least I could do for my poor mother," Scarlett lifted her shirt to show the scars.

"Let's not forget how he was always trying to touch me in 'inappropriate' places... the guy was a drunk pervert!"

"Shit, I have to go," Claire realized she was out of time. She walked to the table and took a one last bite, before heading for the driver waiting outside. "Quickly, drive back to the hotel," she ordered.

Claire tapped at the sensor by the room door; the door was opened. She quickly changed her clothes and shoved the bag under her bed. It was five; and Claire now has three hours to rest before Michael wakes her up.

"Just you wait, Michael. Soon, soon enough, you will feel the true meaning of being alive..." mumbled Claire, while slipping in under her cozy blanket.

∼

"Wake up students; it's time to go!" Sophia knocked randomly on the doors.

"Claire, wake up. We're running late!" Michael tapped Claire's shoulder.

"Go ahead of me. I'll dress up and follow you guys," replied Claire with a sleepy tone. Michael wore his glasses and jacket, closing the door behind him as he left.

"Alright students, I need you to leave everything distracting you and focus on me," ordered Rachel; she was one of the three professors assigned for this trip. Unlike the other two, Rachel had actually volunteered for this trip. She had close relations with a lot of the students, mainly because of her social skills and a contagious smile on her face.

"Today, we will attend a small workshop. Then, the rest of the day will just be museums. Try to keep up!" beamed Rachel.

Claire finally caught up. She looked around and found Michael standing behind Lucas. "You made it just in time," remarked Michael.

"What's this stain on your hip?" he then inquired.

"Oh, this? Probably nothing," Claire tried to rub the stain off, which appeared like that of some dried blood that might or might not belong to an underaged girl Claire was interacting with last night... "I gotta be more careful," she thought.


The workshop took five hours, with the breaks and whatnot; it was almost one, and the group had arrived at the first museum. "We will meet here in thirty minutes. It's a small museum and shouldn't take more than that to explore," remarked Sophia.

"Michael, let's go," Claire held Michael's stiff hand.

"Wow, look at all these bodies," noted Claire.

"It's amazing how detailed these are," noted Michael.

"They aren't made; these are the real deal!" replied Claire.

"What? How do you know that?"

"Wanna ask that woman?" challenged Claire.

"Excuse me, are those bodies real?"

"Yes, indeed they are," answered the woman standing by the staircase.

"See, told ya," smiled Claire. Michael smiled back then observed these pieces of art.

"So, about last night," spoke Claire with a faint voice.

"Oh, I'm sorry if I said anything weird back then."

"No, the truth is—"

"Michael!" called Lucas. "Are you done yet?"

"Not yet."

"Why does he always show up at the worst time?" Claire wasn't pleased by Lucas's presence. "Lyla, have you guys checked the VR zone on the fourth floor?" She devised at once.

"No, I had no idea they have one. Hey, let's go check it out!"

"All right, see you soon Michael."

"That should keep them busy for a while," thought Claire.

"Claire, were you about to say something?"

"Michael, Claire, time's up. We have to go now," called Sophia.

"Never mind, they're waiting for us," signed Claire. No matter how many times she tries, Claire's attempts to confess seemed to be disturbed. She just wanted to make sure Michael shares those same feelings.

The group finished their museum tour; and the bus terminated at the hotel entrance. "You have the rest of the night for yourselves. But keep in mind, tomorrow we're driving early. Have fun!" remarked Rachel.

"What should we do? I mean it's still seven," inquired Lucas.

"How about the four of us go somewhere to eat?" suggested Michael.

"If you say so," hesitated Lyla.

"Fine by me," answered Lucas.

"What about you, Claire?" asked Michael.

"Huh...oh, yeah whatever," Claire was deep in her thoughts.

"Hey, Michael, there is this Chinese restaurant by the bridge. How about giving it a try?"

"Sure, why not!"

After walking for ten minutes, the group arrived at the restaurant. A Chinese sign was fixed by the entrance. Lucas was first to enter, followed by the rest. "Are you all right? You seem a bit absent minded," Michael asked Claire as she sat down.

"Yeah, I'm just facing a dilemma."

"What kind of dilemma?"

"The kind that you would be embarrassed to share with a friend," smiled Claire.

"As you all know, today is our last day here in London. The flight won't depart until ten in the evening, so we have some time to spare," explained Sophia.

"We thought we could go on a small trip to a forest or something like that. You know, some quality time with nature away from the busy city," added Rachel.

Students started chattering as they hopped in the bus and sat in their usual seats. "Um, professor, I forgot something.

Can I go quickly get it?" asked Claire.

"Sure, don't be late!" approved Sophia.

"I'm sorry, Michael. I just can't see a way around it," thought Claire as she was waiting for the elevator.

Five minutes later, Claire returned; she was holding a small sling bag resting across her body.

"All right, we're ready to go," remarked Rachel; the driver closed the automatic doors.

Michael felt something on his left shoulder, "Um, Clai—" Claire was sleeping on his shoulder; Michael smiled then continued reading.

The bus arrived thirty minutes later; around 1700 acres of trees were covering the place. "Each pair will walk together; we will meet back here in three hours." Lucas and Lyla were the first pair to go; pairs then followed them deep into the forest. Michael's team was the last.

"Claire, we arrived," Michael tapped on her shoulder.

"All right, can you go ahead of me?"

"Something's wrong?" asked Michael.

"I just need to go to the lady's room. Assuming there is any out here." She shrugged.

"Got it, call me when you're done," noted Michael before hopping off the bus.

Claire looked to her right and left; students were deep in the forest, and so were the professors. The driver was trying to take a nap in his seat. "Clear!" she muttered.

She walked away from the group and isolated herself. Facing a lake, she stood still; Claire opened her sling bag and inserted her hands slowly. "It's time you take a break from following Michael everywhere, Lucas!" mumbled Claire as she grabbed Lucas's passport from her small bag. Claire flipped through the pages; she then hopped on a tied boat and went deep into the lake.

"I hope you enjoyed London, because you're staying

here!" laughed Claire as she threw his passport into the muddy lake.

"Hello Michael, where are you now?"

"I'm heading for a lake. What about you?"

Claire's heart pounded, "A lake?"

"Um, yes."

Claire quickly paddled her way back to the land. "I'm standing here by a lake," she noted while trying to catch her breath.

"Great, I'm almost there."

Moments later, Claire glanced as Michael was making his way through the branches. She waved her hands, and he waved his hands back. "Why are you covered in water? And is that mud?" inquired Michael.

"Oh, that, I was walking by the lake and my leg slipped. It'll dry eventually," explained Claire.

A pair of ravens landed on a bench near Michael and Claire. "I've always adored ravens," remarked Michael.

"I'm a raven person myself!"

"About that night..." Claire shifted her tone.

"I'm sorry for ruining the moment," apologized Michael.

"It wasn't your fault," assured Claire. "It was her fault, that Anna..." she thought.

"Ever heard from Anna again?" inquired Claire.

"No, last time was on the plane. Once we landed, I couldn't feel her whatsoever," explained Michael.

"Strange, I wonder why," Claire tried to hide her grin.

"Michael, I know you suffered a lot in your childhood. But don't you think it's time to move on?"

"What do you mean?"

"You can't have these feelings forever. You are a different person now—different than what you were before escaping. Am I right?"

"I guess you're right," sighed Michael.

The two sat quietly and watched the lake; Michael was thinking about what Claire told him. "Is it really time to move on?" he wondered.

# TRUTH

THE STUDENTS RETURNED TO THE HOTEL. THEY HAD TWO hours for any last-minute packing. "It's not here!" snapped Lucas.

"What's wrong?" asked Lyla as she rushed out of the bathroom.

"My passport, I can't find it!"

"What with the yelling?" Michael knocked the door separating the two rooms.

"What do you mean you can't find it? Look deeper into the safe!" snapped Michael.

"I placed it by my bed—here on this table," explained Lucas.

"I'll go inform the professors; you continue to search everywhere. Look behind or under the bed."

"What's going on?" Claire just entered the room; she had gone to the gym in her free time.

"Oh Claire, Lucas lost his passport. Can you please help the boys look for it?"

"Sure! I'll try my best," replied Claire.

"Hey, I heard about your passport. Any progress?"

"No, I searched everywhere!" Lucas was wiping the sweat off his forehead.

"I'm sure it's here somewhere," grinned Claire.

"Lucas, have you found it yet?" Rachel came through the side door.

"No," he simply said.

"I see, I guess we have no choice but to go without you."

"What are you saying professor!" snapped Lyla, "We can't leave him alone here!"

"It's all right, Lyla. I can deal with this myself. I'll go to the embassy and—"

"Then I'm staying here with you!"

"Are you sure about that?" asked Rachel.

"Yeah, I can't return knowing he's not with me," Lucas's heart pounded.

"Lyla, you can't stay here. What about your grandparents? They will surely be worried. Plus, you have to start studying for the midterms," remarked Lucas; as much as he wanted Lyla to stay with him, he knew she had to return back.

"Fine but promise me you will keep me updated."

"I promise..."

"You gonna be alright by yourself?" asked Michael.

"Yeah don't worry, It's not my first time going to an embassy," winked Lucas; Michael smiled, then walked to Claire.

The lobby was quickly filled with students. They checked out and saw the bus approaching the entrance. "Good luck, Lucas," muttered Michael as he hopped on the bus.

"Hey, calm down, will ya!" Claire placed her hands-on Michael's lap. Michael stopped shaking his lap and cooled down.

"Sorry, I tend to get all worked up when things get out of my control," explained Michael.

"Look, I'm in no place to judge you; but don't you think

life is more complicated than to have it 'under control?' I mean you were prisoned in your house, right? Now that you are encountering the real world, believe me, you will find all sorts of people," remarked Claire.

"I guess you are right. You know, just last year, Lucas and I were competing for Anna. But after her death, fate managed to make us best friends."

"I'm sure most of you noticed, but Lucas won't return with us. He has some issues and will return back soon," said Sophia.

"Shit!" snapped Claire.

"Claire?"

"Um, is it possible for us to return to the hotel?"

"Forgot something?" asked Rachel.

"Kind of…"

"I'm sorry, I think there is no way back. Is it that important? You can ask Lucas to bring it with him."

"No! Never mind," smiled Claire.

Lyla watched the hotel as the driver drove away, "Lucas," she muttered.

"HI, I just checked out, and would like to check in again."

"Absolutely, for how long?" asked the receptionist.

"Um, I think a week—not sure though," hesitated Lucas.

"All right, that'll be nine hundred fifty quids. Would you like to pay upfront or when you checkout?"

"I think I'll pay when checking out."

"Sure, I just need a fifty-pound insurance payment." Remarked the receptionist with a smile. Lucas handed him the money then remembered, "Can you give me my old room?"

"I'm sorry, that room is booked; although, I can give you

the room beside it, the one where your white-haired friend used to live."

"Fine I'll take it."

"Great, now if would just give us some time to clean the room—"

"No!" snapped Lucas. "I don't mind taking it as is."

"You see, I'm a bit tired and could really use a nap right now." He added with a light chuckle.

"Most certainly. Here is your room card. Enjoy your sta—"

Lucas grabbed the cards, thanked the guy, then rushed to Michael's old room. "Stop, no need for housekeeping," ordered Lucas. He entered his new room and started looking around for his lost passport. He looked on the tables, and underneath them. Lucas then sat on his knees in an attempt to reach under the beds.

His hands touched something, "Strange," he muttered. Lucas pulled his hand away from the bed. "A bag?"

"It seems someone forgot their bag here," thought Lucas. He slowly unzipped the bag, "gloves, empty container, and some papers."

"No name ID, damn it…" Lucas unfolded the first paper, "It's some sort of map," he thought.

Lucas knew the embassy would be closed by now; and since he had some free time, Lucas wanted to return the bag to its owners. Before heading out, he unfolded the other paper. "It can't be!"

He shoved the other paper in his pocket, then headed to search for a taxi. On the way, Lucas tried to think about what he saw on that piece of paper. His thoughts were interrupted by the driver who kept asking for directions.

After arriving, Lucas paid the driver then walked to what seems to be a warehouse. Lucas glanced at an opening in the fence, "There!" he thought.

"It stinks in here..." As he was looking around, a cooler box grabbed his attention. Lucas approached the box, and slowly opened it.

"Wha—" Lucas felt something coming out of his mouth; he tried to swallow it, but the vomit found its way out.

"What the hell are those?" Lucas wondered. He closed the box at once then tried to cover any traces he might've left behind. He walked for five minutes before finding a cab.

"What's going on? Why where their bodies in that box? Whose bodies are those? And who stored them in here?" Lucas had a lot to process.

The taxi stopped by the hotel entrance. Lucas got out and went directly into the hotel. "Sir! You haven't paid yet!" remarked the driver.

"Sorry," apologized Lucas as he handed the money.

"Those bodies, they were cut into pieces; some were missing more parts than the others. I can't deal with this right now; first my passport, now this... I want to sleep," Lucas couldn't concentrate on his priorities. He returned to his bed and closed his eyes; the very bed that had a bag stashed underneath it...

MICHAEL'S FLIGHT arrived at Dubai International Airport. The students dragged their luggage to the arrival's hall. Michael was worried about Lucas; he wanted to call and check on him, but it was 4AM back there.

Students said their goodbyes and went of their separate ways. "Let's go!"

"Just a sec," said Michael. "Lyla!" he called out.

Lyla turned around to find Michael running to her. "Are you going to be all right?" he asked.

"I'm fine, my grandfather is waiting outside."

Michael and Claire went up the escalator to the metro platform.

Ten stops later, Michael stood up, "I guess that's my station. See you tomorrow!"

"Yeah... Hey, thanks for being my partner... I really appreciate it," smiled Claire, and so did Michael, to a lesser degree that is.

Michael unlocked the door and entered the apartment. "Finally, home..." It was a Saturday morning, and Michael had nothing to do. He had just arrived from a six-hour flight. Michael thought the best thing to do now is have a cold shower, then attempt to sleep.

"I'm out of pills!" snapped Michael; he immediately dialed his psychiatric number. It was out of service. He then called the number provided in their website. "Hello, I would like to make an appointment."

"Absolutely! Someone in mind?" asked the woman.

"Yeah, Dr. Thomas."

"I'm sorry, he's on a sick leave."

"Fine, who else do you have? Someone who's willing to meet me now."

"We currently have two who are free now: Dr. Ahmad and Dr. Tiffany."

"Um, I'll go with Tiffany."

"Excellent, when can we expect you?" inquired the woman.

"I'll use the metro, so maximum thirty minutes," explained Michael.

"All right, may I have your name?"

"Michael... Michael Walker."

"Great, Mr. Walker. See you soon." Michael hung up; he quickly dressed up, then walked to the station nearby.

"Good morning, Michael. My name is Dr. Tiffany and I'll be your therapist until Dr. Thomas returns."

"Nice to meet you," smiled Michael.

"So, what caused you to come?" asked Tiffany.

"Um, where should I start?"

"From the beginning…"

"I grew up in a rich family, but didn't enjoy my life—felt something was missing. I had everything except the thing that makes me wanna wake up the next day motivated: freedom."

"And did you achieve this 'freedom' you aspired for?"

"I did, but the cost was heavy on me. I lost a lot in the way to my freedom. Anna was a friend who accompanied me in this journey, she died from a brain stroke. My father died in an accident. My mother lost both her eyes. I had this fiancée that my father had on me. I ran away the night before our wedding."

"I'll be honest with you... I never lost a close friend not to mention a relative, so I can only imagine how horrible you might've felt. But the way I see it, you had nothing to do with their deaths. I think you are blaming yourself just because of something inside of you—something that feeds on your guilt," explained Tiffany.

"You know, I took psychology once in high school, and now I'm taking a more advanced one as an elective. My mother was a great psychiatrist who helped a lot of people. What I'm trying to say is that I'm not sure whether therapy is the answer at this point. I need a new approach to this situation of mine."

"The question is, do you feel like satisfying this urge? Or do you want to fight it? To stand against it."

"I think that Anna's death made me the guy I am now. I'd never linked my soul with another being, except for her. She was a tool that turned to have a huge place in my heart. I never thought I'd lose someone this dear to me. It was after she died that I started seeing therapists and took those pills."

"What sort of pills?"

"I can't remember since I took them out their package and placed them in a container. But I'm sure they were anti-depression pills," explained Michael.

"Oh yeah, speaking of Anna, I started experiencing some vivid dreams where she would come to me as a spirit."

"Interesting…what do you think she wants?"

"I-I'm not sure. I think she was trying to warn me of something. But then I'm not sure if it was really her or just my brain playing games on me," remarked Michael.

"I think this needs more than one session. What exactly did you discuss with Thomas?" inquired Tiffany as she was doing some paperwork.

"I only told him about Anna's death and how it affected me, he immediately gave me those pills."

"Well, Thomas isn't the best here, frankly speaking. He wasn't always serious about his work," remarked Tiffany.

"Listen, stop taking those pills, and take another appointment with me. I have another patient in ten minutes, but I really wanna know more about what you are facing."

Tiffany's phone rang, "Sorry, I have to take it. See you soon!" Michael nodded as he walked out of the room.

"I never thought therapy could be this helpful. I feel better now. Well, better than I was before coming here at least…" thought Michael.

# ALLURE

"Hey Emily, open up! It's me," knocked Claire.

The door was opened, and Claire entered a small apartment in an old building. "Welcome back, Luna!"

"Hey, we have a new target!" remarked Claire.

"Is that so? And who might 'it' be?" inquired Emily curiously.

"That's her. I've been stalking her for a while, and now is the perfect opportunity," Claire pulled a photo from her pocket.

"She's cute! I wonder how her upper arms would taste if I slow cooked them," remarked Emily.

"I want you to do your thing, and make sure she's ready to consume by tomorrow. I have a special dinner coming up..." grinned Claire.

"All right, leave it to me!"

"Anyway, it's way past midnight, I have to go. Oh yeah, wrap her ribs for me, I'll cook barbecue ribs for my guest. The rest you can save for later."

"A guest?" inquired Emily.

"You'll meet him soon. Right after I make him lose hope in this society," laughed Claire.

"Oh yeah, how's Scarlett? Is she coming or what?"

"She doesn't want to leave her stupid mother. But I think it's good to have two locations. After all, we can't secure this place forever!" remarked Claire before heading out.

Claire was walking in Dubai's night streets when her phone rang, "Who would call at such time!" wondered Claire. "Oh, It's Scarlett," Claire tapped on the 'answer' button. "Yello!"

"Luna, did you by any chance leave your bag in the warehouse last time you visited?"

"What? No, I brought it back to the hotel—"

"SHIT!"

"What?" asked Scarlett.

"I forgot it in my room. How did it end up in the warehouse?"

"You forgot the bag in the hotel! Are you crazy?" snapped Scarlett.

"Relax will ya! It's not like it had anything important," Claire couldn't think straight.

"So, someone must've taken the bag to our hideout. Is that what you're saying?" yelled Scarlett.

"Listen, it's three and I'm on my nerves. Why don't I think about it then give you a call later today?" offered Claire.

"Fine but try to be more careful for God's sake!"

Claire hanged the call and rushed back to her apartment. "Who? Who found my bag? And why would he leave it in the hideout?" Claire laid in her bed unable to sleep. Her mind was busy trying to figure out how her bag ended in the warehouse. She managed to squeeze in four hours of sleeping time; she was awakened by her 8AM alarm. Claire switched on the lights and went to take a cold shower.

In the metro, Claire sat in the 'woman-only' zone. She started reading her new book as the metro went past one station at a time. The metro stopped at a station, and Claire lifted her eyes to glance at Michael entering the next cabin. "Michael!" Claire greeted, as she walked out the woman-only cabin.

"Oh Claire, how are you doing?"

"I'm doing great! Ready for uni after a long vacation?" Claire initiated the conversation.

"Well, the midterms are coming, no time to rest now!"

"Say, um, you free tomorrow evening?"

"I think so, why?"

"I'm cooking dinner and was wondering if you'd like to join me."

"Sure, I'd be honored!"

"Great, I'll send you my location. You can come around eight thirty," remarked Claire as she was texting Michael the address. "I look forward to our dinner tonight!" She then added with a subtle grin.

～

THE FOLLOWING DAY, Michael returned back from his class; he dressed up then rushed to Claire's place. "I think this is the place," he thought, standing before a relatively old building. Michael walked to the apartment number mentioned in Claire's text; he took a deep breath, then knocked the door.

"Yes?"

"It's me, Michael."

"Oh, just give me a sec!"

Michael heard unlocking noise; before finally, the door was fully unlocked. "Wow, that was a lot of unlocking," he chuckled.

"Yeah, it's just what a girl living alone would do," smiled Claire. "Come on in!"

Michael walked into what seemed like a small apartment with a bedroom, kitchen, bathroom, and a average sized living room. "Have a seat," offered Claire.

"Smells nice in here."

"I thought I'd BBQ some ribs for our dinner!" stated Claire as she sat the dishes on the table. She then poured two glasses of red wine and placed one on each side of the table. "There you go," Claire placed half of the rib on Michael's plate; she placed the other half on hers.

Michael grabbed a knife and sliced a small piece. Claire watched closely as he picked the piece with his fork and aimed for his mouth. Michael took the first bite. Claire waited for a reaction, but Michael's face had the same expression. He took another bite. Still nothing.

"So? What do you think?"

"It tastes great! I've never tasted such tender meat before," Michael was amused by Claire's cooking skills.

"Glad you love it," Claire finally took a bite from her plate.

Michael licked his dish empty, and Claire was enjoying this girl's meat slowly. She knew girls like her were hard to find.

After dinner, Claire and Michael moved to a small sofa faced by a 32" TV. "So, any news on Lucas?" inquired Claire, settling into her portion of the sofa.

"I think he'll need a couple of days before they give him a new passport," explained Michael.

"I see... well it must've been hard for him, alone in London," remarked Claire.

The silence resumed in the room; Michael's heart was racing, and so was Claire's. "Michael, I—"

Michael's phone rang; it was Lucas. "I'm sorry, I have to take this," Michael walked to the door. "Hello?"

"Michael, good news! The embassy said my papers should be ready in three days."

"That's great, so I guess we'll see you soon then."

"Yeah... by the way, have you seen Lyla?"

"Now that you mentioned it, she didn't come to yesterday's class," stated Michael.

"What?" snapped Lucas.

"Relax, I bet she was tired from the trip. She'll probably come to tomorrow," assured Michael.

"Anyway, I tried calling her phone, but no one answered. If you find her, tell her to call me."

"Will do," said Michael before hanging up.

"Who was it?" asked Claire.

"It was Lucas," replied Michael.

"Is he all right?"

"Yeah, he's fine. He'll be back in like four days. Anyway, I really enjoyed our dinner tonight, but I think I need to head back. I'm sure you know how the streets are after eleven."

"All right, I'll see you around!" smiled Claire; she stood up and walked towards Michael. Claire kissed Michael; he couldn't back off, not with the door right behind him. Michael closed his eyes and tried to live the moment.

"That was our first true kiss!" She winked. Michael smiled back then closed the door behind him as he exited.

"Wait, could it be that Lucas has something to do with the bag Scarlett found? I guess I just have to wait," Claire stood by her window and watched Michael walking into the darkness of the night.

DAYS WENT by as Michael awaited Lucas' promised return. Not knowing where Lyla was, Michael grew worried. He asked her professors, but no one had seen her since landing in Dubai. Michael didn't want to worry Lucas, so he kept her status hidden from him, for now at least.

Michael sat in their living room, with the calculus book in his hand. He didn't want to waste any more time waiting for Lucas; midterms were two weeks away, and Michael wanted to maintain his record this semester as well.

Fifteen minutes later, the door was unlocked from outside, "Michael, I'm here," called Lucas as he pushed his bag through the door.

"Welcome back," Michael closed his book and placed it near him.

"So, have you reached Lyla yet?" asked Lucas the moment he sat foot into the apartment.

"About that, she still hasn't showed up…"

"Are you serious? Did you ask students about her?" Lucas tried to call her phone one more time.

"I asked all her professors, no one knows where she is," explained Michael.

"Damn it, she's not answering," yelled Lucas.

Lucas then remembered what he found in Michael and Claire's hotel room. "Michael, I just remembered another thing."

"But before I start, I want you to have a seat. And keep in mind I'm not entirely sure about what I'm about to say," remarked Lucas.

"After you left along the rest, I checked in once again. They gave me your old room, since mine was booked. While I was looking around for my passport, I bent down to check under the beds. I reached inside and felt a bag."

"Then?"

"I grabbed the bag from underneath, then opened it. Found some papers laying around, and what seemed to be an empty container and a pair of gloves. One of the papers had a map. I went to where the map was marked. I arrived at a worn-out warehouse. After sneaking in, I found a cooler box. I opened it and found what can only be expressed as 'big body chunks'."

"What!" snapped Michael.

"I quickly escaped and left the bag behind," continued Lucas.

"So, how is this connected with Claire?"

"Take a look at this," Lucas unfolded the second paper that was in the bag. "Remind you of someone?"

"It's just a small girl who appears to be with her sister," noted Michael.

"Look closely. Does this scar look familiar?"

"No! It can't be," snapped Michael; Lucas nodded slowly. "Still, this can't prove everything..."

"Then what about the fact that I found the bag in your room under her bed?" yelled Lucas.

"We can't just blame her based on our assumptions."

"Michael, open your eyes. This girl isn't normal. There's a reason why people are avoiding her." Lucas sat down, "Hey, remember when we went to the movie with her? My stomach was fine until Claire offered me a drink. I had to spend my evening in the bathroom. Also, if you think about it, there is no way a passport could just vanish into thin air," Lucas threw everything he had; he couldn't think of anything else to accuse Claire with.

Michael stood up and walked to his room, "I'll talk to her tomorrow; thanks for warning me." Lucas remained seated in the couch; he knew that Michael had feelings for Claire. But he also knew that as his friend, he had to be honest with Michael. His mind was split between Lyla and Claire.

Michael couldn't sleep; Lucas's words were swimming inside his head. "Is that true, Claire? Is that the real you?" he wondered.

After lying in bed for ten minutes, Michael had made up

his mind. He grabbed the jacket lying on the floor then walked towards the door.

"Where you going?" asked Lucas.

"I'm going to confront Claire."

"Now?"

"What other choice do I have, HUH?"

"Fine, then I'll go check on Lyla," Lucas stood up.

"You know where she lives?" asked Michael.

"Yeah," replied Lucas while wearing his shoes.

"All right, good luck."

"Good luck to you too…" said Lucas.

# DIVULGE

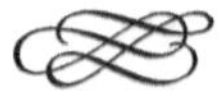



"Michael…"

Claire opened the door, "Is everything all right?"

"We need to talk…"

"Wanna go for a walk?" offered Claire.

"Sure," approved Michael.

Claire led the way; they walked for five minutes before she started the conversation. She knew that Michael knows something; therefore, Claire wanted to set the mood first. "By the way," she said, "you weren't the only one who suffered in his childhood. I was bullied in school; not the regular bullying, but the kind that leaves a mark. I was literally tortured every day. My parents? Living in their small perfect world. They didn't bother to help, not to mention, believe me…"

"I'm sorry to hear that."

"That was just the beginning. This stuff led to what the therapist diagnosed as a 'disorder'. My parents began fearing me. They thought I might be a bad model for my little sister." Michael had nothing to say. His past can't compete with

Claire's. At least he lived a luxury life; she couldn't afford a normal life to start with.

"Ever since, people were afraid to talk to me. Rumors spread I was a psychopath whom her parents failed to raise. My parents realized I could threaten their jobs, or even their social life," Claire paused to wipe her tears. "Guess what, they kicked me out of the house! Who would kick a sixteen-year-old girl?"

"I had no idea you suffered this much. I—"

"It's all right... I moved on after giving up faith in this society. I wondered why isn't anyone helping me? Why was I isolated from the rest? After living for a while in my friend's house, I finally gave up to my inner demon—"

"Your inner what?"

"You know, the voice you hear deep inside you," explained Claire, then continued, "I was seventeen when I allured my little sister to the woods. A voice told me to get revenge—to take what my parents treasured most... Their youngest daughter."

"I took her along with my friend deep into the woods. We'd promised her a beautiful pond while in reality, I stabbed her heart with a kitchen knife."

"What!" Michael snapped.

"My body was moving on its own. I ripped her skin, and then ate whatever I could slice. Scarlett, my friend, was showing a shocked face, before ultimately joining me."

Michael's face turned pale, "How could a calm girl like Claire have such past? I've read a lot about similar cases of revenge; but eating her sister! This is insane," he thought.

"I bet my parents sobbed at their 'missing' daughter for a few days, before moving on with their lives."

"So that photo, it was you!" Michael started to lose focus. "What photo?"

"The one Lucas found in the bag you had hidden under

the bed. He told me about the warehouse, and what was in that cooler box. I couldn't believe him—I convinced myself that this wasn't you."

"So, he found it, didn't he..." muttered Claire.

"Michael, I had a reason. And so did Scarlett..." spoke Claire. "She was even more abused than I. Her father would whip her along his friends just for fun. Her body was covered with scars. Afraid of him, her mother ignored her daughters suffering. Scarlett then realized this had to end," explained Claire.

"Wait don't tell me—"

"Yup, she killed her father. I helped with the eating."

"How can you be this cold-hearted? Do you realize that you are eating humans?"

"Do you still have feelings for humans? We both know how greedy they get. I'm not saying that we aren't humans; I guess we just evolved over the average human level," explained Claire.

"But still, don't you think this is wrong?"

"Honey, you just ate your friend's girlfriend. Admit it, wasn't it the best you ever had?"

"What are you talking about?"

"The dinner, three days ago, that was Lyla!" sang out Claire with a creepy smile up her face.

"What!" Michael shoved his finger into his mouth; he was trying to vomit any leftovers of Lyla. Claire grabbed Michael by his shoulders and kissed him.

"It's gonna be all right," she whispered in his ears.

"You killed Lyla... You killed her!" yelled Michael as he backed away from her.

Claire grabbed his once again, "Just surrender yourself, and everything will be all right. Listen to your inner self—be one with it!" Michael started to cool down; his shivering body stopped moving. He looked into Claire eyes; tears slipped on his cheeks. Claire hugged him, her body was squeezing on Michael's.

"Why don't we return to my place? Hmm? I can pour you a glass of wine, and we can talk with no one to hear," Claire had Michael under control. Her soft voice tamed Michael's anger and gave him no choice but to give in.

"Morning!" rejoiced Claire.

"What happened last night?" Michael was wiping his wet eyes; he had to sleep in Claire's apartment, for his body couldn't help him back home, not after their conversation.

"How are you feeling?" asked Claire.

"Strange," replied Michael. "I never felt this before. For long as I can remember, I never opened my true self to anyone," added Michael.

"I'm sorry for lying to you before. I just thought you would be afraid of me. Just like everyone else."

"You know I would accept you no matter what! No matter how you look, no matter what people say about you, I would love you for what's hidden inside," smiled Michael.

"Thanks."

Michael heard his phone vibrating; it was placed on the table across the room. Claire hurried to the phone and declined the call. "Who was it?" asked Michael.

"Don't worry about it," she placed the phone back on the table.

Michael snapped, "Lucas! He was supposed to check on Lyla last night."

"Well, we both know he ain't finding anywhere," laughed Claire.

"I have to return to him, otherwise he'll get suspicious," noted Michael as he stood up from the couch.

"Fine, but you have to come with me tonight."

"Where?" inquired Michael.

"I want you to meet my group," added Claire.

"You have a group! I thought it was you and that Scarlett girl."

"Nope, we were five. Unfortunately, one had to be eliminated."

"What?"

"She had it coming. That girl, Jocelyn, was plotting against me since we first met. I bet she wanted to take my role as a leader."

"Oh, and by the way, we only eat girls—the younger the better. Just like the one you had that night," explained Claire with a calm face.

"The party isn't until midnight, so you have a whole day to study," remarked Claire.

"Fine, I'll come…" said Michael with a sigh.

"Hey Michael, listen. You are a smart guy, try to act accordingly," said Claire as Michael was closing the door.

Michael arrived at his apartment; he opened the door to find Lucas sitting on the couch eating his breakfast. "Michael? What happened, man? I tried calling you since last night. I went to Lyla's house; her grandparents didn't see her for the past four days. They reported her missing to the local police,"

Michael's heart pounded, "I-Is that so?"

"Lyla…" mumbled Michael; he couldn't believe that he ate her.

"So? What happened last night?" asked Lucas.

"I… I went to pick up Claire. We had dinner in a restaurant, then returned back to her apartment. I got dizzy and she offered me to spend the night there," explained Michael.

"What about the portrait? What about the bag? She's a monster! Don't let your feelings cloud your logic."

"I think it's just a big misunderstanding. After all, the girl in that photo had black hair. Think about it, someone came before us and forgot his bag—it can happen," Michael tried to cover up for Claire.

"Still... Never mind, I'm glad she wasn't who we thought she was." sighed Lucas then continued his cereal.

Michael head directly to the bathroom for a quick shower. Lucas wasn't convinced at all; it was obvious that Michael was hiding something, and Lucas wanted to find out what it was.

IT WAS ALMOST MIDNIGHT; Lucas was heading to his bed when he saw Michael wearing his shoes. "Going somewhere?"

"I'm going for a quick jog. It became kind of a daily habit."

"I've been living here with you for over a year, never have I saw you going for a run!"

"I started when you were still in London."

"Fine, but why this late?" asked Lucas.

"Well, I guess I love the streets at this time. It's quiet, and there's this cool breeze that blows by," remarked Michael.

Lucas wanted to follow him; but his body hadn't recovered from the jet lag yet.

Michael went to Claire's place using the late metro and waited by her door. "You're early," said Claire while unlocking her many locks.

"I was lonely. Anyway, where is this party?"

Claire unlocked the last lock and opened the door, "We tried to blend with this society as much as possible. Sometimes we go to a local disco; other times we head for a 'darker' disco. And rarely, we just hang around in an apartment."

"I see," said Michael as he entered and sat on the couch.

Claire was finally ready; she wore her black shirt, and a white face mask.

"What's with the mask?"

"You want one?"

"N-no," hesitated Michael.

"If you say so. Anyway, we have to get going," remarked Claire.

"How are we gonna get there?" inquired Michael.

"A taxi, of course," laughed Claire; she waved at the only taxi roaming around, "go there," she handed a paper with an address written on it.

Michael had no idea where he is headed to; for all he knows it could be one of the three places Claire mentioned.

"So, it's the dark disco, huh" thought Michael as he got out of the car. Claire paid the driver before leading the way into the building. It was a dark basement with speakers scattered ten feet apart. Deafening Gothic music was streamed through the speaker, and people ranging from sixteen and up to twenty-five were seen dancing and mingling.

"Why am I the only one with a white shirt?" asked Michael.

"Relax, no one will notice. Plus, you are 'the new guy'—they'll understand," replied Claire.

"Hey, Luna!" waved Emily while walking her way through the dancing teens.

"Emily that girl…DELICIOUS!" sang Claire; Michael felt a pinch in his chest. Eating Lucas's girlfriend was one thing; but not telling him… The immense guilt was wrapping his heart.

"Emily, this is Michael. The guest I told you about," remarked Claire.

"Hi, I'm Emily, nice to meet ya!"

"Is she drunk?" whispered Michael.

"No, it's just how she's," whispered back Claire.

"Say, where is Sarah?"

"Oh, she is over there, with her boyfriend."

"Her what!" snapped Claire.

"What's wrong?" inquired Emily.

Claire rushed to Sarah and grabbed her from the back. "Claire! Glad you could make it—"

"What did I say about bringing outsiders? And a boyfriend, really?" whispered Claire with notable anger in her tone.

"Excuse me, Jorge, I'll be right back," said Sarah. She walked away from her boyfriend then continued, "What's the big deal? He doesn't know about our secret. Didn't you encourage us to blend?"

"Yes, I told you to blend, but not bring a stranger to our meeting!" snapped Claire.

"Oh yeah? What about that guy over there? He's with you, isn't he?" Sarah pointed at Michael who was talking with Emily.

"Michael's different—he's one of us."

"So, your friend is okay and mine is not? I thought this 'cult' is only for girl-eating girls."

"He ate his best friend's lover! Can your friend over there do that?" Sarah didn't respond. "I bet he can, he used to go hunting with his father," challenged Sarah.

"Fine, why don't we make sure?"

"What do you mean—"

"Hey, Jorge? Hi, my name is Claire. I'm friends with Sarah. Wanna come with us? I have something cool to show ya!"

"That'll be great!" smiled Jorge.

"Shall we?" Claire winked at Sarah then went to inform Michael and Emily.

"Where are we going?" asked Michael.

"Just trying to prove something," grinned Claire; she called a driver she knew as the rest were gathering outside.

"Jorge, why don't we call it a night? It's getting late, we don't have to go," begged Sarah.

"It's all right, they seem cool."

"Damn it!" muttered Sarah. Jorge and Sarah were the last two to exit the building; the rest were already settled in the car.

"Go to the apartment," ordered Claire.

The car was packed; Claire beside the driver, Michael by the window, and Jorge between Sarah and Emily.

# MISFORTUNE

THE APARTMENT WASN'T THAT FAR; IT WAS AN EIGHT-MINUTE drive from the disco. "All right, we're here. Ready, Jorge?"

"Ready!"

"You guys go ahead of us. Emily, let them in, while I talk with Sarah out here," remarked Claire.

After Claire made sure the rest went into the building, she flicked her eyes to Sarah. "Here is the deal, either he consumes the girl and be part of us. Or he vomits, and his head will be the next thing to fall out of his body!"

"Are you serious! What happened to only killing girls?" snapped Sarah.

"Well, it was your idea. I merely approved it," Claire showed a maniac smile. Sarah's face turned pale. She stood still in her place; her body couldn't move, knowing her boyfriend was going to be killed.

"Come on, they're waiting for us!" sang Claire as she walked ahead. Sarah took a long breath before finally walking behind Claire.

"Sorry for they delay."

"So, what you got in here?" asked Jorge.

"I know you're excited. But believe me, there's no need to rush things. We have all night long!" smiled Claire, before strolling to the kitchen along Emily and Michael. Jorge and Sarah sat on a couch.

"Jorge… run!" whispered Sarah desperately.

"What? Why—"

"All set!" called Claire from the kitchen.

Jorge rushed to see what the hype was about; Sarah sat in her place. She didn't want to see her lover's head get chopped. As metaphorically as it may sounds, Sarah knew Jorge was a dead man one way or another. Sarah met Claire two years ago, and she didn't joke about this sort of stuff.

"Are you ready?"

"Oh yeah I am. What ya got?"

Claire grinned before opening the fridge; a head rolled and fell on the floor.

"Whoa!" snapped Jorge.

"Lyla!" exclaimed Michael, immediately reaching down to grab Lyla's head from the floor and hugging it. "I'm sorry Lyla… I had no idea," he mumbled.

"So, what do you think?" asked Claire.

Sarah rushed to the kitchen, "Jorge, you alright?"

"It-it's a body—a dead body!" he finally snapped.

"You're crazy…y'all crazy people!" Jorge tried to head to the door which was blocked by Claire.

"Where to, sweetheart?"

Jorge looked at Sarah, "What's going on?"

"I'm sorry, I tried to warn you. This is the real me," Sarah said with a sigh. She took off her hijab; her white hair finally saw light.

"Your hair, it's white!" stammered Jorge.

"Listen big guy. You have two choices," noted Claire. She then walked to Jorge; he tried to back off but got stopped by the wall behind him. Claire sat her hand on the wall, right next to Jorge's head. "You can either join our little group or be part of it; Literally!" Claire offered her two options.

"Jorge—" hesitated Sarah.

"Shut up and let him think!" snapped Claire.

Jorge looked around him; he saw three girls with white hair and a guy standing by the corner. "Damn it…" he muttered.

"I-I'll join you!" Jorge gave his answer.

"Smart." said Claire as he sliced a piece of Lyla's liver. "Come on, eat!" she poked it against Jorge's face.

"Oh god…" muttered Jorge as he grabbed the piece off the fork. Jorge stared at his hands, then at those strangers staring at him. He closed his eyes, then shoved the piece into his mouth. Jorge had no time to taste it; he didn't even chew but swallowed it immediately.

"Welcome aboard!" said Claire.

"Sarah…" mumbled Jorge.

"Jorge," Sarah hugged Jorge.

"Claire, it's getting late. I told Lucas I'm going for a walk," remarked Michael.

"Is that so? Fine, you can leave. The driver is waiting outside," said Claire with a sigh.

Michael rushed to the driver and returned back to Lucas. "Good, he's asleep," thought Michael as he locked the apartment door.

"Thirty minutes after midnight, interesting…" muttered Lucas from under his blanket.

It'd been almost a week since the last time Michael tasted human flesh; his last meal was a dear friend of his, Lyla. She was Lucas's lover, and took part in their communication class group. Michael had to hide this new identity of his from the people around him. Neither Lucas, nor his therapist, Tiffany, should know about it.

"Michael, time to go," called Lucas.

"Alright, coming," answered back Michael.

"I can't believe this… Lyla's still missing after nine days," sighed Lucas. Michael didn't respond.

"You know, I don't think Lyla would disappear like that on her will. I bet she was kidnaped," added Lucas.

"I'm sure she is alright."

"Say, you still hanging with Claire? I know she's hiding something."

"I think you are exaggerating. She works with me in the group, can't just cut her off!" explained Michael.

"Alright, my class is this way," noted Lucas.

"I'll meet you after class," Michael took a left turn.

"Michael!" called Claire from the other side of the room; she was alone. Michael checked his phone watch; the class doesn't start for another ten minutes. He walked to where Claire was and sat on the seat beside hers.

"So, how much does Lucas know anyway?" she inquried.

"He knows that Lyla is missing. Oh yeah, and he doesn't trust you at all," remarked Michael.

"As long as he believes that we're gonna be alright," assured Claire.

"What now? We just go and kill girls for food?" asked Michael.

"Look, it's not like we have no social lives. We just meet every couple of days to consume someone. Then, each member is on their own," explained Claire.

"Why don't you meet me at my place tonight?"

"What about Lucas? I can't lie to him every time we have to meet."

"Then don't! Just go out when he falls asleep."

"Fine, I'll meet you after midnight—maybe by one. He usually goes to bed by midnight."

Sophia entered the room, "Morning Michael, Claire."

"Um professor, about Lyla—"

"Yeah, I know. I hope they find her soon."

Michael returned back to his seat as students entered the classroom. Sophia waited for the rest of the students to arrive. After the class was full, she stood up from her chair and said, "How was the holiday? I know it's only seven days, but I'm sure it was refreshing."

"Now, that we are back, let's continue with our chapter. But first, I would like to remind you about your group assignment. It's during our next class, which is on Tuesday," added Sophia.

LATER THAT SAME DAY, Michael was getting ready to meet Claire. Lucas, as usual, faked his snoring as he waited in the bedroom for Michael to leave.

After Lucas heard the door closing, he quickly jumped out of the bed and glanced through the window; he could see where Michael was heading to. "Where are you going?" he wondered.

Lucas exited the apartment and followed Michael. It wasn't the first time Lucas had to stalk Michael; since he came to Dubai, Lucas stalked Michael more than once. He recognized Michael's pattern; how fast he walks, and how often he turns around to check his surroundings. Michael entered the metro station; he tapped onto the sensor then went right. Lucas had an open pass, so he just had to keep an eye on Michael from behind regardless of where Michael was heading.

Michael exited the metro after eight minutes, Lucas

followed him while making sure to keep a distance. And as Michael rushed up the staircase, Lucas was right behind him.

"Open up," whispered Michael as he knocked the door. In the meantime Lucas was hiding behind the stairs while maintaining a close distance between them.

"Claire!" muttered Lucas. "Why would Michael meet her after midnight?"

Michael entered and Claire locked the door. Lucas wasn't sure whether to get closer or give up and go home. He grabbed his phone and started taking random photos; the street, the door, and the whole building. "This isn't over, Claire. I'll come back for you," thought Lucas; he then got on the same cab that brought him here and head back home.

"That was close," sighed Michael.

"You have to be more careful. He isn't that dumb," remarked Claire.

"So? Why am I here?" asked Michael.

"Remember that guy, Jorge?"

"That muscular guy we met last time?"

"Yeah, I don't trust him. But I can't get rid of him."

"Why?"

"Well, he is Sarah's lover. Also, we need a muscle man in the group!" grinned Claire.

"So?"

"I want you to keep an eye on him for a while."

"You know I can't. Also, what can I teach him anyway?"

"Just hang out with him, as a friend. See if he's a threat. Or just do what guys usually do, hang in a bar!"

"I'll try…" sighed Michael.

"Great, take his number. You can call him tomorrow," Claire handed Michael a piece of paper.

.   .   .

THE NEXT MORNING, Michael tried calling Jorge before heading to his class. He called one time, then another time; Jorge didn't respond. Michael then called Claire to make sure he got the right number. "What do you mean he isn't responding?"

"I tried calling him more than once. Why don't you ask Sarah to check on him?"

"No! She can't know about this. Listen, I'll send you his address, go check on him after class."

"Fine," said Michael before hanging up.

"Michael," Lucas tapped on Michael's back.

"Don't you have a class?" asked Michael.

"It got canceled. The professor is having a baby!" explained Lucas.

"I see… Well, enjoy your day off!"

Lucas walked past Michael and towards the main exit. "I haven't slept well last night; I should go probably go take a quick nap," he thought.

# ALONE

Back in Brierley Gen Avenue; Lisa was sitting in her office, as usual. Lately, she had nothing to do; certainly not after getting blind by that accident. "David," she called.

"Yes madam," David entered the office.

"Call this number," Lisa handed over her phone.

"There you go," David returned the phone, having dialed said number.

"Now leave and close the door after you," ordered Lisa, and David nodded out of habit.

"Olivia? Hi, this is Lisa—Rita's friend."

"Hi Lisa, Rita told me about you."

"Is everything alright?" inquired Olivia.

"I need something only you can help me with."

"What is it?"

"Do you still have those 'connections' with your dealer?"

"Yes, why?"

"I want some hydrogen cyanide."

"What!" snapped Olivia.

"Can you please get some and come by tomorrow morning?"

"Wait, what are you—"

Lisa hanged the phone, then called David. "Tomorrow morning, my friend will come by to visit. Make sure to welcome her to my office."

"Very well…" replied David.

The next morning, Olivia came and found Lisa sitting by her desk. "Olivia, is that you?" asked Lisa.

"Yes," answered Olivia.

"David, will you leave us alone."

David closed the door; Olivia walked and sat on the chair in front of Lisa's. "Lisa, what's going on? Why did you ask for a poison? Are you—"

"Olivia, I can't do this anymore. This whole being a widow with no sight— it's just stressful. Sure, my husband left me all his fortune; but what's the point of having money if you can't see it?"

"Are you saying that you want to end your life just because you can't see anymore?"

"It's more complicated than that, dear. I can't fulfill my role as a human being. This suffering, is not worth living for," Lisa's eyes began to tear.

"Listen, last time I helped a friend, I ended up messing their whole marriage. I don't want to be the cause of another family to tear down."

"This family is already torn down," remarked Lisa.

"Don't say that, you—"

"No one is left for me—they're all gone!" snapped Lisa.

"You know what, you're a smart woman. I'll ask this one last time, are you sure about giving up your life?"

"Yes, I'm sure…"

"Then I won't stand in your way," Olivia placed a small tube in Lisa's hand. "Good luck," she muttered before heading out.

"I'm sorry, Isabella, mommy can't be with you anymore." Lisa opened the tube and drank it whole.

"Goodbye, cruel wor—"

~

DAVID WAS GETTING ready to pick up Isabella from her school. He dressed up, then went to inform Isabella's blind mother, Lisa. She was in her home office relaxing alone, or so he had initially assumed. Ever since the time Larry was buried, Lisa felt like isolating herself from people around her. David would take her on a walk in the park, and that was it. She would sit by her office for rest of the day before David would walk her to bed. "Madam," David knocked on the door; but she did not respond.

"Lisa?" David knocked once again, but Lisa didn't respond. "I'm coming in," he finally opened the door which was surprisingly unlocked.

"MADAM!" David snapped as he rushed toward her. She was resting on her chair with arms open to both directions. Her eyes were shut, and her mouth was slightly opened with some sort of foam dripping out. David tried to shake her; she didn't respond. He then noticed a small recording device Lisa used with her patients. David opened her fingers slowly, then took the device from her hand.

*"I never thought life would be meaningless with no eyes to see its beauty. How funny is it to motivate people while in fact, you are depressed? I assuming that David is the first one to hear this recording. David, I'm sorry I left without saying goodbye to you and Isabella; I just thought my depressing face would scare you off. Anyway, Isabella won't take this easily, try to comfort her; let her feel safe around you."*

David pressed on the next voice file:

*"This next recording is for Michael; only Michael can listen to*

*it. David, I know I'm asking for too much; but can you go with Isabella to check on Michael? I'm sure he would be happy to meet you after a long time. Isabella's school are having a holiday in two weeks, you can go by then."*

David stashed the recording device in his pocket, then called the cops.

"Earl, go pick up Isabella," called David from inside the room.

"Why? What's going—"

"Oh my god, madam!" snapped Earl as he entered the room.

"Hurry up, I've already called the police," ordered David.

Earl hurried to Isabella's school; he parked near the entrance and watched as students exit with their parents holding their hands. "Found her!" thought Earl, eyeing young Isabella.

"Miss Isabella, over here."

"Earl? Where's David?" Isabella threw her bag inside then sat down.

"Um, he ran into some problems. Meanwhile, why don't we go to the ice cream shop?"

"Earl, I'm not a kid anymore."

"Sorry, then where do you want to go?"

"Home," replied Isabella with a cold face.

"It's still early, we can go shopping If you want!" offered Earl.

"Is everything all right? Did something happen?" inquired Isabella at last.

"I just thought we could change your daily routine. I know how strict David can be," chuckled Earl.

"Fine, then drive to that new mall."

"You got it!" smiled Earl.

Earl stalled Isabella for five hours or so, before David called him back. After arriving home, Earl hurried to his room; Isabella was welcomed by David, who was waiting by the door.

"Isabella, we need to talk," said David. Both walked to Larry's study room; David unlocked the door, then switched the lights on.

"Come, have a seat," he offered.

"Your father was a good man," remarked David. Isabella looked around the room; it's been almost a year since the last time she's been here.

Isabella then realized what was going on, "Say, where's mom?"

"About that—"

"Where is she!" yelled Isabella.

David hugged Isabella then said, "She went to your father —to a better place.

Isabella took her time in crying; losing both parents while she was still fifteen. David pulled the device out of his pocket then played the first track. Isabella sobbed as she heard her mother's last words.

"Listen, Isabella, I'll always be there for you; and no matter what happens, I want you to be the strong girl I know."

"Why? First Michael, then dad—and now..."

"It's all part of fate. You just have to keep marching on without looking back."

"Speaking of Michael, you and I are going to visit him." remarked David.

"What? Why?"

"Don't you miss your big brother? I know things weren't going smoothly between you two, but you're still his sister."

"But—"

"We'll go after the funeral."

Isabella returned to her room, while David went to talk with the butlers. "Earl, open up."

"So, what was the cause of death?" inquired Earl.

"They said she drank some poison called hydrogen cyanide."

"To be honest, I can't blame her. She lost her son and husband, and now she's blind. It must've been tough for her," remarked Earl.

"I suppose so…" sighed David.

LUCAS AWOKE FRIGHTENED and above all sweating like crazy; he was worried about Lyla's whereabouts. He dressed up before heading out. "It's still five, I have to start somewhere," he thought.

Lucas ended up at Lyla's house. He knocked the door; her grandfather opened the door showing a brief inquiring expression.

"Oh, Lucas!"

"Good afternoon Mr. Ali, I have a question regarding Lyla."

"Of course, come on in!"

Lucas walked in and followed Ali to the living room. There, he was offered a cup of tea along some traditional sweets. "So, what did you come for?" inquired Ali.

"Before Lyla went missing, did you notice anything strange?"

"Strange, you say… I can't say I have," hesitated Ali.

"I know this might sounds weird, but can I check for something in Lyla's room?" requested Lucas.

"I guess you can," approved Ali. Both went upstairs to Lyla's bedroom. Lucas began by scanning the room with his eyes; he aimed for anything unusual. Lucas then walked around while still searching with his eyes.

"What's that?" he picked a folded paper off the desk. He unfolded it, "Could it be…"

"What's wrong?" inquired Ali.

"I'm not sure; but I think I have a lead," remarked Lucas, bending his knees to search under Lyla's bed, and behind her desk.

"What are you looking for?" asked Ali.

"Lyla's phone."

Lucas felt something behind the desk, "Found it!"

"Why would she hide her phone?"

"What does it say?" Lucas pointed on the paper.

"Dear God! This is a threatening letter… It ordered Lyla to leave her belongings here and go to this place," remarked Ali, taking the paper from Lucas and read between the lines, "Wait, they threatened to kill us if she didn't show herself in thirty minutes!"

"Shit! I'll go check that place—"

"Let me go with you," begged Ali.

"I'm sorry, you can't. It's hard to hide the two of us. But don't worry, I'll keep you updated," explained Lucas.

Lucas took a taxi to the address written on the paper. Once arrived, he realized he was in the middle of a street; buildings were lined up both sides. Lucas turned around to find a building; it was right next to a small supermarket. He entered and went to the guy guarding the place.

"Hi my friend gave me her room number, but as you can see, I can't read Arabic. Can you show me which room is hers?"

"Sure, let me see," said the guard, "third floor, room thirty-seven."

"Thanks!"

"Room thirty…seven…" mumbled Lucas as he was looking at the rooms to his right. After finding room 37, Lucas brainstormed his next move.

"Should I knock first? What if Lyla is tightened to a pole or something," Lucas finally made his decision. He walked back a few steps. Then, with all his force focused on his shoulder, he ran into the door. "I did it!"

"Lyla, you in here?" Lucas then walked through the rooms, one after another; there was no sign of any living being. He reached the kitchen and saw a huge pool of blood on the floor; right next to the fridge.

"Oh my god!" Lucas avoided the blood and reached the fridge handle.

"What the—" He jumped back, landing on the blood puddle.

"It's just like London—wait, could it be? Claire!" Lucas tried to cool down; he had no choice but to close the fridge door and get out of here. As he was pushing the flesh inside so the fridge can be closed, Lucas noticed a head with blonde hair.

"No, it can't be!"

"LYLA!" Lucas held her head to his chest, as his eyes wept of pain and sorrow…

# DOUBT

Michael went to check on Jorge; he hasn't answered any calls, and Claire began to doubt the info she had received from Sarah regarding where Jorge's whereabouts. "Jorge? Jorge?" Michael knocked the door with no answer. "What if..." he tried to open the door; it was unlocked. He entered the room and started looking around aimlessly.

"Shit—Jorge!"

"Hello, Claire!" Called Michael.

"What? I'm in class." Whispered Claire,

"It's Jorge. he's dead!"

"What?" Snapped Claire.

"There's vomit all over the place, and a dead body by the couch. I'm sure he's been like this since last night at least," explained Michael.

"Just lock the door and wait for me. I'll be right there," remarked Claire. Michael snapped some photos of the body, then locked himself inside the nauseating apartment.

Twenty minutes later, Michael heard a knock on the door; he peaked through the peephole. "Finally," Michael opened the door at once.

"I called the rest. Emily has some business to take care of and will meet us in the main hideout. Sarah is on her way," noted Claire.

"Look," spoke Michael, "I doubt he died a natural death, or that someone killed him."

"So, you think it's Lyla?"

"Think about it. It was his first time, and he ate a raw liver. Livers are packed with Vitamin A—usually, too much of it can cause heavy vomiting," explained Michael.

"Then how come I never threw up?" inquired Claire.

"I have to guess it's because you got lucky a couple of times. I got lucky too…"

Sarah opened the door and marched in. "Where is he?" she yelled.

"Shh! He's here," whispered Claire.

"Jorge!"

"Step back! Don't touch him," snapped Michael.

"Don't tell me you were behind this Claire. He did exactly what you told him. Why did you kill him?" She sobbed.

"Sarah, I didn't kill him. Okay?" responded Claire with a serious tone.

"Then how come he died mere days after you met him?"

"I don't know, probably cause his body couldn't handle a raw human liver," remarked Claire with a shrug.

"And whose fault is that!" Sarah couldn't hold her tears.

"We have to wipe out anything we might've left traces on," remarked Michael.

"Someone should call the cops. We can't leave him like this," sobbed Sarah.

"Yeah, someone other than us… We have to get the hell out of here, now!" ordered Claire.

"Emily should be done by now. Let's go meet her at our hideout." Claire and Sarah exited while Michael checked for any traces of them. He followed them after making sure nothing was left behind.

"Wait," called Michael. "I think it's dangerous to leave the body here."

"What do you mean?" asked Claire.

"The forensic team will probably notice the intensive amount of Vitamin A in Jorge's body. Therefore, they can trace it to an 'unknown substance' he ate days before dying. In our case, a human liver," explained Michael.

"Then what do you suggest we do?"

"We have to get rid of the body. I know you've never done this before, but the forensics won't cross over the human liver part. This could put us all in danger!"

"But how?" inquired Sarah.

"What you do with a body after killing it?"

"It's usually Scarlett and Emily that take care of this sort of stuff," explained Claire.

"Then call Emily. We don't have much time."

~

LUCAS WAS SOBBING over Lyla's head. His tears poured over her frozen hair, and his legs shivered as her head sat still on his thigh. "I have to go, but first…" he grabbed his phone and called the police.

After cleaning after his mess, Lucas retreated out of the apartment and walked to the nearest metro station. "Michael, you're dealing with the devil's daughter!" thought Lucas.

EMILY WAS on her way to the apartment; she had some business to attend to. Her phone was silent, but Emily could feel it vibrating in her pocket. "Hello?"

"Are you free now?" asked Claire.

"Yeah, I'm heading to the apartment."

"Change of plans, come to Jorge's place. I'll send you the location," ordered Claire before hanging up. Emily checked her phone for the location and went to where it pointed.

"Claire? Is everything all right?" asked Emily as she entered the apartment.

"We want you to get rid of the body," noted Claire.

"What?"

"I know it's hard for you, but we have to," remarked Michael.

"Alright, I count on you. The rest, let's go to the apartment," dictated Claire. Sarah wore her hijab then walked behind Michael and Claire.

As they were approaching the apartment, Michael noticed police cars parked right in front of the building. "Are those—"

"Stop, don't go any further," ordered Michael.

"What's going on? Why are the cops in the building?" asked Claire.

"It seems like your 'hideout' is no longer valid. We need to escape," noted Michael with a sigh.

"Anyway, let's go to my place before the police notice us." The three took a cab back to Claire's apartment. There, they tried to think for a way to escape without causing any extra mess.

"I say we go to Scarlett," suggested Claire.

"Wait, I can't just leave Dubai! what about the university? What about Lucas?"

"You think this is a good time to worry about your boy friend? Huh? I bet he has something to do with this!" exclaimed Claire. "I guess London's our only option..."

"Fine, you go, and I'll follow you later," offered Michael. "I wasn't connected to you guys directly. So I doubt they'll find anything against me…"

"Sarah, go home and prepare. I'll call Emily. Book tickets for you two. Michael and I will join you later," explained Claire. "Michael, Lucas is probably wondering about your whereabouts. Go home and be there for him."

MICHAEL HURRIED BACK HOME to Lucas, who was cleaning himself. "Lucas, I'm ho—"

"Is that blood!" snapped Michael.

"Michael, I found her… I found Lyla…"

"You found Lyla? Where?"

"It was Claire…" mumbled Lucas.

"Speak up, I can't hear you!"

"It was Claire! SHE killed Lyla!" Lucas finally exploded.

"Lucas, take a deep breath, then tell me exactly what happened."

Lucas sat down on with the blood stain on his back. He took three deep breaths then said, "I went to Lyla's house and found a letter. I found an apartment filled with bodies, just like the one I found in London. And then, Lyla's head was shoved in a refrigerator." Lucas paused to wipe his tears.

"Then? Did you call the cops?" inquired Michael

"I did," replied Lucas.

"I'm sorry for Lyla. If only I knew about her location sooner, none of this would've happened," Michael forced a couple of tears out.

"Are you still denying Claire's connection to all of this?"

"I guess you were right all along," sighed Michael.

"What are you going to do about it? I told you Claire was bad news."

"So now what? Should we report Claire to the cops?"

"Too bad it's not this simple." Noted Michael, "Do you

have any solid evidence that proves she killed someone? If not, then no one will take you seriously."

"Listen, it's getting late. Why don't we sleep and discuss this tomorrow?" suggested Michael. Lucas walked back to his room without uttering a single word; he tried to block the tears.

"Claire, we can't risk Lucas finding out about us. He called the cops back there. He's up to something... Until the heat gets a bit cooler, we'll only text—no meetings whatsoever. Got it?" Michael sent to Claire.

THE NEXT MORNING, Lucas went to his class, while Michael stayed behind. He didn't feel like going to class today. Claire ceased the opportunity and visited Michael. "Michael, open up!" she knocked from outside. Michael opened the door slowly; his eyes were still sleepy.

"Don't tell me you didn't sleep last night?"

"I tried but couldn't. The most I slept was two hours." Michael wiped his eyes then locked the door after Claire.

"Have you read the newspaper yet?" asked Claire, as she was opening an article online.

"You know I don't read Arabic."

"Anyway, check this out," Claire handed her phone over to Michael. He in return took a minute to scroll through the page, "It's about your hideout…"

"But don't worry, they didn't find anything. Well, other than the corpses. Oh and Emily, she managed to get rid of that Jorge guy."

"We have to make our next move soon. I'm not sure how long I can keep Lucas out of this," noted Michael.

"The problem is we can't just disappear. People will

wonder. I hate to admit, but I made some 'relations' here in Dubai," explained Claire.

"You're right—wait, what are you doing!" snapped Michael.

"I'm sure you're stressed, maybe even more than I am," Claire pulled a wrapped needle out of her purse.

"Are you insane!"

"It's nothing serious, just some heroine—helps to relax your stiff body," Claire inserted the needle slowly into her right arm.

"Sto—"

"Too late!" smiled Claire. "Now... It's your turn," she grabbed Michael's hand.

"Claire, wait—" the needle entered Michael's body through his veins.

"Do you feel anything?" asked Claire.

"Damn it! Why would you do—" Michael stopped talking; his body was giving in to the injection. He sat on the couch and closed his eyes.

"There you go... Now relax and let the potion do its magic!" Claire turned off the lights, before joining Michael on the couch.

LUCAS RETURNED HOME after finishing his two classes for the day. "Michael, I tried calling you. Did you skip class?" Lucas was still trying to unlock the door from outside. After finally opening the door, Lucas was faced with a huge puddle of vomit covering the couch and floor.

"What happened in here?" wondered Lucas; he then heard a flush sound from the toilet.

"Michael? You alright buddy?" Lucas knocked the door.

Michael opened the door, "Lucas?"

"What with all the vomiting? And what's wrong with your

eyes?" Michael rubbed his eyes, then walked past Lucas and into the bedroom.

"Michael, wait!"

Michael locked his door with no respond. "What's with him?" wondered Lucas. As Lucas was cleaning after Michael, he glanced on a something stashed behind the couch.

"A needle?"

# FLIGHT

TWO WEEKS HAVE PASSED, AND MICHAEL WAS STILL LOCKED IN his new room. He had moved his bed to a different room; a desperate attempt to isolate himself from Lucas. The university had sent him several warnings, which he ignored. He'd only open the door for Claire; and she would bring some girl's corpse for her and Michael to munch on. Lucas tried to keep a close eye on Michael; chiefly due to the midterms coming up—he had ultimately failed to find the source of Michael's depression.

"Do you want more or is that enough?" asked Claire.

"That's enough. Also, what exactly is this?"

"Emily said it's from the back area. I think she mentioned something about it being near the ribs," explained Claire.

"Why are you still doing this? The apartment was found. Where are you guys even killing the girls?"

"Oh, Emily borrowed a storage unit from her friend."

"I'm telling you, things are getting risky here. The cops are taking this matter seriously!" noted Claire with a mouthful.

"Then why the fuck do you keep killing those girls!"

"Come on! This meat is worth the risk."

"Well, the cops are closing in."

"I think it's time for Plan B."

"What's Plan B?" asked Michael.

"London, our second hideout. Scarlett's already there, so that's one more member to help!"

"London you say, alright… But we have to work fast. Lucas is getting closer with every passing day. The last thing I want for him to know is that I ate his girlfriend."

"I have no problem going to the airport this instant! What about you? How soon can you be ready?" inquired Claire.

"Um, I think by tomorrow morning…"

"Great, I'll check for flights and book mine. Then I'll send you the flight number so you can book on the same flight," remarked Claire.

"Fine, but I think you should leave. Lucas will come back any minute now."

"Alright, I'll keep you updated."

"By the way, since when do you wear a hijab?" asked Michael.

"Oh, this, it's just a way to blend in—to be a bit less suspicious."

Claire took the empty containers and was on her way out. Lucas had just exited the metro station; the apartment was in his sight. He saw a woman wearing all black exiting his apartment. Lucas stood behind a streetlamp and kept her within his eyesight. The breezy wind reviled some white hair from beneath the hijab. Lucas noticed white hair strands slipping out and could only think of one person. "Claire! Why is she here?" he wondered.

After making sure the way was clear, Lucas hurried to the apartment. "Michael!"

"Oh Lucas, you're back."

"What's wrong with you?"

"Nothing, I'm fine," replied Michael calmly.

"You can't just skip classes—the midterms are next Sunday!"

"Is that so?"

"Hey, I know a lot of crazy stuff happened recently, but you can't just run away. You'll have to face them, eventually," Lucas placed his shoes near the door, then went to his room.

It was almost nine in the evening; Michael began packing his suitcase. He folded some shirts, and a couple of pants. Shortly afterwards, his phone vibrated; it was an email from Claire with her flight confirmation. Michael booked his flight, which departed at 7:00AM sharp. "I've got to get some rest. It's going to be a long day tomorrow..." thought Michael.

In the next room, Lucas was thinking about Claire. He had no solid proof that she killed Lyla; but deep inside, Lucas knew she did indeed kill the poor girl. "I just need a proof—maybe a picture or even recorded footage. But how?" wondered Lucas as he drifted away into deep slumber.

"WE'RE FINALLY HERE! That flight sure was tedious" laughed David; Isabella attempted to smile but couldn't.

"Um, do you know where Michael is?" she finally spoke.

"Now that you mentioned it, I have no clue!"

"So, what are we going to do? It's almost eight, and I barely had any sleep." Remarked Isabella.

"Well, I guess we can spend the morning in some hotel, then start searching later today," recommended David.

"Okay—"

"Next please" called the police officer.

"Come on, it's our turn," noted David.

After clearing the immigration process, David spotted

their luggage rolling to the moving belt. "You wait here, I'll go call a taxi," ordered David.

"Why not use the metro?"

"A metro, huh? But we don't know where to go."

"I just looked online. There is a famous street where most of the hotels are located," explained Isabella.

"Very well, let's go."

MEANWHILE LUCAS AWOKE by the sound of his 8AM alarm. "Michael, time to go; this time you're coming no matter—"

The living room was empty. Lucas opened Michael's door, but no one was in there. He then tried calling him, but Michael didn't respond; his flight has already left. There was no trace of Michael in the room. His room hasn't changed since the last time Lucas entered it. Everything was right in its place; except Michael's suitcase and backpack. "Wait, did he actually leave? Without leaving a letter at least!"

"Damn it, I can't think straight. I need breakfast." Lucas grabbed his phone and head straight to the metro station.

"Let's see…" muttered Lucas; he stood in front of the metro line map.

Since the class doesn't start until 9:30AM, Lucas thought he could go to that cafe he always frequented.

In the metro cabin, Lucas stood near the door; the cafe was only few stations away.

"Lucas?"

Lucas turned his face to find an old man with a little girl. "David!" he rejoiced.

"Do you know him?" inquired Isabella.

"He's Michael's friend, Lucas."

"Hold up, what brings you here?"

"To be honest—"

"My mom died… No, our mom died, me and Michael."

"Oh my god! What happened?"

"It's a long story, and we haven't eaten for a while now," remarked David.

"I'm heading for breakfast, come join me," offered Lucas.

The three exited at the next station and went to the cafe. Lucas sat in front, facing both David and Isabella. "Lisa lost her eyes in a car accident. Apparently, she couldn't handle her depression and gave up."

"So, suicide?"

David nodded, then looked at Isabella; she had a cold face on.

"By the way, where is Michael?" asked David.

"That's an even longer story," sighed Lucas.

"Well, we have nothing else to do," smiled David.

"It all started in London..."

Lucas told them everything about Claire, Lyla, and all that was tangled in between.

"So, you're saying that this morning he just vanished?"

"Yeah, his bags were missing—meaning he's somewhere."

"Why didn't you stop him!" snapped Isabella. "If you knew all along that he's in danger, why didn't you stop him, HUH?"

"I'm sorry…"

"I'll go to him. I can't afford to lose another family member," spoke Isabella with determination, after having cooled down ever so slightly.

"But Isabella, I have to head back, there is a lot of paperwork to go through," noted David.

"It's all right, you can return. I'll be fine by myself."

"What do you mean by yourself?"

"I can't trust Lucas. I'll go alone."

"You're just a child! You can't even book a flight!"

"Lucas, can Isabella stay with you?" begged David, knowing how determined Isabella can be.

"Alright…" sighed Lucas.

"My flight is tomorrow, ten in the evening. I'm going to have to find somewhere to sleep for the night." Noted David

"Then come with us, my apartment isn't far away."

"I have a class, so we have to head back now," added Lucas.

After arriving, Lucas handed David a spare key, then rushed to the cab waiting outside. "Oh Isabella, you can stay in Michael's bedroom," he yelled from downstairs.

David opened the door, "So Michael lives here... Not bad!"

Isabella walked around the place, she then entered Michael's room. "It stinks in here..." She brushed the dirt off Michael's bed and picked the pillow off the floor.

"David, I'm going to rest for a while."

"Fine, I'll rest here on the couch," replied David.

"HEY, SCARLETT," texted Claire.

"Luna, where are you?"

"I just called the driver, he should be here any minute now."

"Great, I'll meet you at the warehouse..."

"Just texted Scarlett," remarked Claire.

"Wait," realized Michael, "where is Sarah?"

"Sarah? She changed her mind last minute. Don't worry about her, she knows *almost* nothing."

Both hopped into the black sedan, "Go," ordered Claire.

Claire's phone vibrated in her hand, "Interesting..." she muttered showing a maniac grin.

"What?" asked Michael.

"Nothing, I just figured out an old joke that I didn't understand," Claire returned her 'normal', usual smile.

The drive lasted forty five minutes, before they both arrived at the warehouse. "Luna, took you forever to come!"

"Claire, glad you made it safely," said Emily.

"I'm back! Emily, does Scarlett know about the new developments?"

"Yes, she told me what happened," remarked Scarlett.

"So this is the place Lucas mentioned," thought Michael, scanning his surroundings.

"Oh, you must be Michael! I was eager to meet you ever since Claire first mentioned you," Scarlett offered a hand-shake; Michael shook her hand.

"Where are you planning to stay?" inquired Scarlett.

"I guess we could find an apartment," noted Claire.

"Can't they stay with us?" inquired Emily.

"We can't all stay with my mom!" remarked Scarlett.

"It's all right, Emily," said Claire, "You stay with Scarlett. I'll manage a place for me and Michael."

"Anyway, I think we should get going," Both Claire and Michael returned to the car parked outside.

"Now what?" asked Michael.

"Now we go to my parent's summer house!" answered Claire with a grin.

"Your parents have a house? Here in London?"

"Yup."

"To the summer house," ordered Claire.

"Scarlett, drop Emily and wait for me at our place. I'll let Michael do the check-in and come to you," texted Claire.

"Fine, I'll drive Emily home, then go to the park," replied Scarlett.

Claire then sent one last text, before returning her phone back to her purse. "Listen, Michael, I have somewhere to be. Here are the keys, feel like home!" Claire handed the keys as Michael exited the car.

"Raul, go to that park," Claire pointed on the car screen.

Claire arrived first; she walked around the park, before finally reaching the small lake. The sun was already gone, and the moon reflected its glow on the water. Claire squatted in an attempt to touch the water. "It's been a while since we met here," spoke Scarlett from behind.

"I know it's sudden, but I had to talk to you—alone…"

Scarlett walked and sat next to Claire, "Well, I'm here now."

"I found a new target. Well, Sarah did."

"Who?"

"It's going to be a tough one, but I bet the taste will make it worth our time."

"Ooh?"

"Our little bird told me that Michael's little sister is in Dubai right now…"

# SANCTUARY

As David made his way back to Los Angeles; Isabella decided to stay with Lucas to find her mischievous brother. It was the midterms week, and Lucas had just finished his third exam. He managed to keep a good record during this last semesters. Unlike Michael, who stopped going to classes a month ago. Lucas now has one last exam remaining; in the meantime, he promised Isabella to take her somewhere for lunch.

"Isabella, I'm home. Let's go get lunch."

"What took you so long?"

"Hey, math is hard!"

"Whatever, let's go." ordered Isabella.

"I wanna go to that huge mall—"

"I don't blame Michael; you're so demanding! Why not just eat in that restaurant by the station?" sighed Lucas.

"Listen, I've been here all morning. At least let me enjoy my only trip of the day," argued Isabella.

"Fine, fine…"

"Oh and by the way, it's called *Dubai Mall*," added Lucas.

After arriving, Lucas and Isabella walked a bridge connecting both the station and the mall. "It's huge!" remarked Isabella as she began wondering around the semi-crowded place.

"Listen, we have to return early. I have an exam tomorrow," noted Lucas.

"You have the whole evening to study. But don't worry, I'll make it quick."

"You know what, we'll eat first, then you go do your shopping. I'll stay behind revising the notes on my phone." he suggested, "Now, where do *you* wanna eat?"

"Hmm... how about that restaurant. It looks cute," pointed Isabella.

"Cute? What about the food? You don't judge a restaurant by its cuteness!"

Isabella was already approaching the restaurant. "Hey, wait," Lucas followed her inside.

"Good afternoon—"

"A table for two please," interrupted Isabella.

"Right this way," said the waitress.

The two settled in their seats, then took the menu handed to them by said waitress. "I think she needs a kid's menu," joked Lucas.

"Shut up!" Isabella snatched the menu and began flipping through the pages.

"What will you have?" inquired Lucas.

"I don't know, maybe cheeseburger... maybe pasta." She shrugged.

"Well, I think I'll take the double cheeseburger." The waitress nodded while writing on her fancy ordering tablet.

"Then I'll have the pink sauce pasta," said Isabella.

"Will that be all?" asked the waitress.

"Oh, and orange juice," remarked Isabella.

"What about you, sir?"

"Um, no drinks for me."

Lucas opened the notes he had on his phone and thoughtfully scrolled through the many equations. Moments later, Isabella saw a girl wearing a hijab approaching their table; the girl pulled a seat and sat between Lucas and Isabell, at the head of the table.

"Excuse me, who are you?" asked Lucas.

The girl took off her hijab; her white hair covered her eyes.

"Are you—"

"Shh, I just want to talk," whispered Sarah.

"What do you want?"

"I'm sorry about your cute girlfriend—"

Lucas stood up, then grabbed Sarah by her shirt; he was ready to throw a punch or two. Isabella stood and pulled him away.

"Listen, I'm here to help!" exclaimed Sarah.

"How can I know you're telling the truth?"

"You don't! Though, I can give you some helpful hints to find Michael."

"How do you know his whereabouts?"

"Let's just say he's with Claire."

"What! Claire?" snapped Lucas.

"That's right… After our hideout was blown, they decided to escape," explained Sarah.

"Where did they go?"

"Sir, your order." The waitress placed both plates then walked away. Isabella dug in, while Lucas had already lost his appetite.

"They went to London," added Sarah.

"London, of course!"

"Anyway, I can't risk talking to you in public. And you,

little girl, do the right thing…" Sarah winked as she wore her hijab.

"We need to go, now!" whispered Isabella.

"What? I have an exam tomorrow."

"I don't care, we know where Michael is."

"Listen, let me finish my exam, then we can go. Also, do you even have enough money?"

"Hey, my dad was LA's district attorney. I'm pretty sure a trip to London won't be a problem," remarked Isabella.

"Then it's settled, we'll go the morning after my exam," Lucas was finally able to regain his appetite due to a sudden surge in his overall excitement.

"Michael, wake up."

"Claire?"

"It's time."

"Time for what?" Michael was fully awakened.

"Our little sanctuary," grinned Claire.

It was 1AM, and Michael had no idea what she meant; he put on a long-sleeved shirt, then splashed water on his face.

"I'll be waiting in the car," remarked Claire.

Michael hurried to the living room; there, he grabbed his backpack, then went to Claire. "So, what is this all about?"

"It's been a while since we had a meeting—all three of us."

"Three? I thought you were four."

"Well, Sarah isn't as committed as you would want her to be. She's more of a scouter if you know what I mean," explained Claire.

The car stopped by a fairly old building; the paint has been torn off, and people seem to avoid walking near it. "Why are we stopping?" inquired Michael.

Claire stepped out of the car and went inside the building. Michael waited for six minutes, before the main door was opened; three girls with white hair were walking out of it. Claire sat in the front seat, while Scarlett and Emily sat to the right of Michael.

"How ya doing, Michael?" spoke Scarlett as she sat in. Michael showed a gentle fake smile, then looked through the window.

After the car stopped at its final destination; the group exited and walked to the warehouse. "Hello, anyone here? Help, I've been kidnapped!" yelled a British teen who was tied to a wooden chair.

"Shhh, it's going to be alright…" assured Scarlett. She then untied the cloth wrapped around her eyes. The girl opened her eyes to four uncanny strangers.

"W-who are you? And what do you want from me?" she hesitated.

"We're a bunch of 'freaks' society had abandoned." Began Claire, "And you, sweetie, is our way to take revenge."

Scarlett then grabbed a small kit hidden under a table. "Luna, I can't wait anymore!" she unzipped the bag and grabbed an eight-inch stainless steel knife.

"Wait!" snapped the little girl.

"The girl's right, Scarlett; we have to prepare the room," laughed Claire.

"Oh right, I almost forget," Scarlett took a wrapping paper and covered the floor around the chair. She then locked the warehouse doors after checking for any intruders. Finally, Scarlett distributed a full white coat with a face mask.

"Sorry Michael, we're out of clothes. Guess you just have to stay away from the action!" sang Scarlett.

"Actually, I don't mind giving him mine," volunteered Claire.

"It's all right, I—"

"No, I want you to have a closer look. See the falling intestines, smell the flesh, and lick the blood!" Claire handed over her white coat. Michael anxiously wore it while still trying to calm his beating heart. After taking a long breath, he was ready to approach the girl.

"I'm sorry," he whispered to her before walking to the side. "Aren't you going to close her eyes at least?" He asked the ignorant girls.

"What's the point? It's not that she will remember anything," laughed Scarlett.

Claire was checking her phone while waiting for Scarlett and Emily to prepare the equipment. She got a text message, and it was from Sarah.

"It's done. They should be here any day now!"

"Excellent…" replied Claire.

"By the way, what are we going to do about Lucas?" texted Sarah.

"Oh, don't worry, Emily can handle a guy like him." Claire stashed her phone back in, as Scarlett was getting ready to slice the first slice.

"Emily, hold the girl," ordered Claire; Emily nodded and grabbed the girl from her waist.

"Here we GOOO!"

A DAY after Lucas had officially started his break, he and Isabella booked a flight to London. "Hey, take this."

"What's this?" inquired Lucas; he was still wiping his eyes after sleeping the entire flight.

"It's a message from our mother. She wanted Michael to hear it." explained Isabella.

"Got it," Lucas took the device and placed it into his waist bag.

The flight landed twenty minutes later, and both hurried through the immigration process.

"So, what's the plan? I really don't understand what's going on, but I think we should do something about them."

"I can't do anything right now, not with Michael hanging around the girls in question," remarked Lucas. "We should find Michael and warn him. Then, I can call the police and ambush the rest." He shrugged, having failed to devise a more sophisticated and efficient plan.

"That's the hotel," pointed Lucas. The driver stopped the car; Lucas paid him before helping Isabella with the luggage.

"Hi, we'd like to check in," Lucas slid both passports on the table.

"Absolutely, Mr...Oskar."

"Here you go, sir. Enjoy your stay." Lucas took the two room cards and gave Isabella one of them. Both then took the elevator to the 12th floor, where their room was located.

"Damn it, not again!" snapped Lucas; the room only had one bed, and it was a queen bed. "You know what, you can have the bed; I'll just sleep on the couch," he sighed.

"It's still early," noted Lucas, taking notice of Isabella targeting the bed with her eyes.

"Well, unlike you, I couldn't sleep during a seven hours flight," she explained.

As Isabella was getting comfortable in her bed, Lucas was heading for the door. "Where are you going?"

"I'm not sleepy yet. Thought I'd go for a walk," remarked Lucas before switching off the lights.

Lucas walked aimlessly in London's streets. The sun was nowhere to be seen, and a thick wave of fog covered the view. "Is that..." Lucas rushed to a familiar bridge; the spot where it all started between him and Lyla. Lucas arrived at the exact spot he once stood beside her.

"Damn it!" he sobbed.

As the city put on its night dark blue gown, Lucas closed his eyes for a moment, then opened them. "Michael, where are you? I bet you are with Claire. If only I could remember where that warehouse is," Lucas was lost in his thoughts.

An icy-cold hand touched Lucas's exposed back, "Hello, Lucas!"

# SHOWDOWN

"W-who are you?" Lucas took a step back in utter shock.

"Easy now! The name's Emily."

"Your hair, don't tell me—"

"Yup, I was there. The apartment you found, that was my place. Well, it used to—before you called in the cops you twat."

"Why? Why did you kill her?" barked Lucas.

"Why? To eat her, of course!" laughed Emily. Lucas charged at her, "What are you gonna do? *Kill* me?"

"Just why?" Lucas fell on his knees at once, his body could no longer support the guilt weighing down his chest and weakened knees.

"It's a long story…" sighed Emily. "None of us lived a normal childhood. Some were bullied, others were tortured. Eventually, we lost hope in humanity."

"What does it have to do with eating humans?"

"I don't know… For me, it was by mistake that I saw Claire and Scarlett in action. Instead of killing me, they offered to join them."

"But why Lyla?" insisted Lucas.

"Well... Claire seems to love her. I guess Lyla should be honored."

Lucas clinched his fist; he tried to control his anger before doing something regrettable. "How long have you been doing this stuff?"

"I think for about a year," remarked Emily.

"Why are you here? Why do you guys keep on approaching me?" asked Lucas.

"I guess you are just easy to approach," chuckled Emily, before checking her phone; the text she have been anticipating was yet to arrive. "How about we go grab dinner?" she then suggested.

"I really don't think it's a good idea to eat with a—"

"It's fine, my treat!" insisted Emily.

"Fine," sighed Lucas.

Emily led the way to a restaurant on the other end of the bridge; it was a Japanese restaurant with tables scattered outside, unlike other restaurants in the area. "What will you have?" asked Emily.

"I'm not here to eat. I just wanna talk," noted Lucas.

"What do have in mind?"

"How about you cut the chase and speak about Michael?" demanded Lucas.

"Michael, huh? I guess I could tell you a thing or two. But then, it depends on how much of the truth you want to hear."

"Everything..."

"Fine, remember that time you got stuck in London? Who was behind it?"

"Claire."

"Correct. The reason was to have Michael and Lyla for herself." Emily flicked her eyes to the waiter approaching them, "Yes, I'll have a yakisoba please—"

"Just continue!" snapped Lucas.

"Anyway, Claire made sure you couldn't interrupt her plans. She, but mostly me, kidnapped Lyla and sliced her perfect body—"

"Don't you dare explain!"

"Sorry. Claire ordered Lyla's ribs for a special dinner. And who was the guest?" Emily attempted to conceal the laughter fleeing her unhinged mouth.

"What's wrong?"

"Nothing, it's just funny how naïve you are. That special guest was no other than Michael!"

"What!" Lucas started losing focus, he slammed both hands on the table before him; that in itself was enough to stop him from falling knees first onto the wooden floor beneath them.

"Relax, he had no idea... at least he didn't at first!" grinned Emily.

"You're telling me my best friend ate my girlfriend?"

"Shhh, people can hear us."

"So that's why Michael was acting weird lately."

"Well, depends on how you define weird."

"Where is he now, anyway?" asked Lucas.

"Michael? I'm sure he's eating dinner with Claire—you know, dinner!"

"It can't be, there is no way Michael could do something like that. That's not Michael—you're lying."

"Am I though?"

"Listen, Michael suffered more than you could imagine. His parents lost interest in him being a son and focused on his value as a successor."

"Believe me, I know Michael more than you," challenged Emily. "I bet you were raised in an average family. Studied at an average school, with average friends. And went to an average university in Dubai. Tell me, did you really *suffer*? Your life was molded for you since birth," Emily paused.

"We, on the other hand, took our share of hatred. Claire was kicked out of her house. Scarlett was beaten up by her father… And I lived my life as a forsaken orphan. This is our revenge against society," continued Emily; her phone then vibrated. "I have to take this," Emily tapped on the answer icon.

"We got her!" spoke Scarlett. Emily returned the phone back in her pocket, then showed a pity smile that she didn't really intend. "It's getting late. If I were you, I'd enjoy this magical Christmas evening before heading back to Dubai. Your 'average' mind wouldn't understand any of this—especially what Michael is going through."

Emily picked her small purse then walked into the darkness of this evening. "One yakisoba," said the waiter.

"I'll have it to-go please," sighed Lucas tracing Emily with his eyes as she seemingly vanished.

"I bet Isabella's starving…"

"Isabella, I brought food," Lucas entered the room, after knocking twice, just in case.

"Isabella?"

Lucas couldn't find her in the bedroom; he then knocked on the bathroom, but the door was opened.

"Hi, I just wanted to ask about my cousin, have you seen her exiting the hotel?" asked Lucas.

"Yes, Mr. Oskar. Her sister picked her up some fifteen minutes ago," answered the guard by the entrance.

"White hair?"

"Indeed. It was rather bizarre. But who am I to judge!"

"I see, well my aunt didn't specify who will pick her," smiled Lucas.

"Damn it, was it Emily? And where did they go anyway?" wondered Lucas.

"By any chance, did you noticed what car she had?" he then asked.

"I'm not sure, she must've parked away and walked here."

"Alright, thanks."

"No problem, mate!"

Lucas ran outside and started looking right and left. "Where is she? Where is she!" he muttered.

After running for ten minutes, Lucas had lost hope. He had no lead, just the names of three serial killers; which might not be their real names. He also didn't want to risk getting Michael into this mess. A blue minivan with tinted windows stopped for the red lights. Lucas felt a strange feeling to peak into the passenger seat. "Is that Emily?" the tinted window showed two ladies with white hair.

Lucas didn't want to waste any chances; he waved at a taxi stopping three cars behind. "Follow that blue minivan. We are a big family, and as always, I got left out," joked Lucas; the driver nodded. The lights turned green, and the minivan took a left turn. Lucas's taxi tried to keep enough distance between them.

"Yup, that's Emily," Lucas remembered the route he took last time to the warehouse.

"Please stop here."

"That'll be twenty five quids," noted the driver. Lucas paid then sneaked on the minivan which was trying to reverse parking. He entered the warehouse through the same gap he used last time. Inside, the place was dark and had no signs of people; at least living people.

"I need to take some pictures as evidence," thought Lucas.

"Alright, bring her in!" called Emily.

"I gotta hide somewhere," Lucas tried to find any safe place to hide. He glanced at the dining table with a cover reaching all the way to the floor. Lucas slid under the table, "that should do it." Lucas tried to raise a bit of the table cover to have a better look. "Isabella!" he muttered.

Isabella was blind folded and had a rope tied around her head covering her mouth. She was pulled by Emily and Scarlett into the warehouse. Emily opened the lights, while Scarlett tied Isabella to a cross like metal bar. Her hands were tied to both sides, and her feet was standing on a chair, while her waist was tied to the same bar. "I'm done over here," remarked Scarlett.

"Great, I'll go call Claire," replied Emily.

"Claire? What are they gonna do—are they gonna?" Lucas began sweating; he tried to keep his exhaling low, even though his heart was beating quicker and harsher.

"They're on their way!" Emily took a chair out of the dining table and sat down patiently waiting for Claire and Michael. Lucas tried to move away from Emily's legs; she was inches away from kicking him with her legs. He crawled to the other end of the table; and before reaching it, Scarlett sat and rested her legs deep into the table. Lucas was trapped in the middle of the table, with no way to see what's going on out there.

"Damn it, I want to slice her!" snapped Scarlett.

"Come on, you just killed that girl two days ago! We have to give Michael a chance to experience this satisfaction," remarked Emily.

"Michael?" thought Lucas.

"I guess you're right… After all, we all had to kill someone close to us. It just has this special feeling. The thought of touching a sibling's blood—GOD! Just ask me about it," Scarlett couldn't contain her appetite.

"You're right. I had to kill my greedy aunt!" Emily clenched her fists. "Strange, I felt something touching my shoes…" she noted.

~

"WHERE ARE WE GOING?" inquired Michael.

"It's about time you become a part of our little group," noted Claire.

"What do you mean?"

"You'll see soon," she smiled.

Raul stopped by the front entrance; Claire took the lead as she entered the warehouse, followed by Michael.

"Isabella!" snapped Michael upon meeting eyes with his sister. She attempted to cry for help but all she could was some hopeless screams.

"He's here…" mumbled Lucas, still underneath the dining table.

"Claire, what the fuck's going on?" hissed Michael.

"What do you mean? It's our sanctuary! I killed my sister, and Scarlett killed her father. We have to make sure you have no feelings for those you love," explained Claire.

"I-I can't kill her. She's my sister!" hesitated Michael.

"Don't you hate her—and your family? Her father is dead, her mother is blind. No one will care about her death. Young and tender, she is indeed the perfect target!" exclaimed Claire as she shook Michael's shoulders.

"What are you going to do, Michael?" wondered Lucas. He tried to peek once again from beneath the cover.

"Let me make this easier for you. I'll kill Isabella, and you kill your best friend. He came here looking for you," offered Claire. Michael shifted his eyes to Isabella tied on a cross. He then observed Claire's face; a psychopathic smile was drawn all over.

"Damn it, what brought you here Isabella?" thought Michael in utter distress.

"Will you just decide already? I'm itching over here!" snapped Scarlett.

"Here, Michael… You can do it." Emily walked slowly holding a knife using both hands.

"Michael, listen to me. We both know deep inside you wanna do it," whispered Claire.

"Damn it Michael, do something!" Lucas felt something with his legs. "A rope? Interesting…"

"So, Michael? Your sister, or your true life?" insisted Claire.

"I-I'll do it…" spoke Michael.

"What!" muttered Lucas.

Michael walked one step at a time; he started to hear Isabella's heart beating as he drew closer and closer to where she was hung. "I'm sorry, sis," he whispered.

"For god's sake Michael!" Lucas rammed into Claire with the rope in both hands. He threw it around her neck and pulled as hard as his fatigued hands would permit.

"Lucas! Get the hell off me!" snapped Claire; but Lucas tightened the rope and squeezed more.

"CLAIRE!" Scarlett hurried to rescue her. "Stop it, you'll kill her!" she cried. Lucas kicked her away and continued tightening on Claire.

"Emily!" called Scarlett as she tried approaching Lucas.

Meanwhile, Emily tried to reach for a gun hidden in the bag,

"Michael!" she snapped.

Michael snatched the gun and pointed on Scarlett, "Stop it, Scarlett. Or I'm gonna shoot!" Scarlett slowly retreated as she witnessed Claire's grasping on her soul.

"Luc—" Claire stopped talking. Lucas let go of the rope, then fell on the floor.

"I killed her… I killed a human being," he mumbled.

Lucas then got off the dusty floor, walked to Isabella, untied her, then walked to the main exit warehouse. He passed by Michael, "Really Michael? Your sister?" he barked, before exiting the warehouse.

Scarlett and Emily approached Claire's body, as Michael remained in his spot. She was lying on her side, with rope traces around her neck. "Her heart's beating!" Emily raised her head off Claire's chest.

"Claire!" Scarlett shook Claire's body.

"S-Scarlett?"

"Claire! You're back!" sobbed Scarlett.

"I guess I passed out…" muttered Claire.

"Michael, what were you thinking? HUH?" snapped Scarlett; Michael didn't respond.

Claire was able to stand up with Emily's hand around her shoulder. "Let's go. We can discuss this tomorrow," she ordered.

Michael took Claire from Emily, and walked her to Raul, who was waiting outside.

"I understand, Michael…"

"No, you don't! Killing my sister?"

"How can you still call her by that label? After all what they did to you?" snapped Claire. "Listen Michael, those people aren't your family anymore. I am your new and only family," Claire grabbed Michael and kissed him.

"You messed with the wrong person, Lucas…"

# GUILT

"I KILLED A HUMAN…" MUMBLED LUCAS.

"Lucas, you did the right thing. You saved my life!" remarked Isabella.

"I guess so," sighed Lucas.

"What now? Michael is still there…" inquired Isabella.

"I guess we should have some faith. If that doesn't work, then we just have to move on with our lives. Remember we only have nine days, before I have to head back," explained Lucas.

The driver arrived at the hotel; Lucas paid, and Isabella went ahead of him to the room.


THE FOLLOWING DAY, Isabella heard a knock of the door.

"Who is it?" she asked.

Isabella opened the door to find a university student wearing hijab.

"LUCAS!" yelled Isabella in disbelief.

"What's going on—you're that girl from the restaurant!"

snapped Lucas; his eyes were still puffy, and his robe was halfway tied. "What are you doing here?"

"I want to help your friend..." remarked Sarah. "I know what happened last night."

"But I killed Claire, shouldn't they be—"

"She's alive!"

"WHAT!" snapped Lucas.

"But I was sure—her body stopped moving."

"I bet she just passed out," noted Sarah. "Can I come in? That's of course if you trust me."

"Are you insane! There is no way—"

"Come in," offered Isabella.

"Isabella, what are you doing?"

"I'm sorry, Lucas. At this point, I feel desperate for any help," she remarked.

Sarah walked in and sat on the couch. Isabella sat by her side, while Lucas stood by the door in a defensive manner. "So, what's your big plan?" he asked.

"We have more than one option. First, we can ambush her. The problem here is that she might find us first. Another way to do it is to call the cops. But, we have almost no evidence—and you might risk me and Michael getting caught."

"These can't be our only options!"

"We can convince Michael to come back to us..." suggested Isabella.

"And how do you propose we do that? We can't reach him. Plus, his mind is already rotten with those drugs--"

"DRUGS?" snapped Lucas.

"Yeah," sighed Sarah.

"May I ask why you're suddenly turning against Claire?" inquired Lucas.

"I wasn't always a fan of eating human flesh. At first, I was just a university student with ambitions. My parents kept begging me to socialize more and find a friend or two. I listened to their advice and ended up with Claire. She was the same as I was—abandoned by the students," explained Sarah.

"Basically, you were forced into doing it?"

"At first yes… But then, I started enjoying it. As gross as it might seem, humans are actually tasty!" remarked Sarah.

"So, what changed this?"

"My boyfriend, Jorge… I've only known him for a month, but he really was something else," Sarah paused. "She killed him!"

"Killed him?"

"Well, not literally. But she forced him into eating a human liver, which apparently can have some serious side effects," explained Sarah.

"I knew this had to stop—I won't risk my life for her," added Sarah.

"Um, your phone is ringing," noted Isabella.

"Shit, it's Claire!" snapped Sarah.

"Does she know you're here?"

"No! I never told her."

"I'm gonna answer…" Sarah tapped on the answer icon.

"Hollo?"

"Hey Sarah, how was your flight!"

Sarah's heart pounded, "um, it was great. Some crying babies, but otherwise it was good."

"Great, when can we expect you?"

"Tonight…" whispered Lucas.

"Tonight," replied Sarah.

"Lovely! See you soon," Claire hanged up.

"Damn it, what will I do. I bet she'll kill me for not telling her."

"Relax, try to act normal. Tell her you changed your mind and came as fast as you could," remarked Lucas. "This is your only chance to restore their faith in you…"

"Alright, I have to go."

"Wait, give this to Michael," Lucas grabbed the recording device from his bag.

"I'll try… but I can't promise anything," remarked Sarah as she reached for the door knob.

~

THE SUN SAT DOWN, and Sarah walked into the warehouse alone; her heart was pounding as she entered. "What changed your mind?" asked Claire.

"I got lonely back there," smiled Sarah.

"Well, glad you could make it!"

"So, what's on the menu for tonight?" inquired Sarah. She walked to the dining table and sat beside Michael. Both exchanged a cold eye contact, before Claire interrupted.

"As I told you, our menu escaped. And for some reason, it's getting harder to find cute teens out there," explained Claire.

"Why not change the target?" suggested Michael.

"Believe me, it's different. A girl's meat is way better," remarked Scarlett.

"For now, we still have the remaining of that girl," added Claire.

"By the way, where will you stay, Sarah?" inquired Scarlett.

"No clue, my flight arrived this morning."

"You can stay with us," offered Emily.

"Are you kidding? If my mom saw another white-haired girl, she'll literally get a heart attack! Plus, we have no extra space," argued Scarlett.

"Why don't you stay in Luna's hotel? You can book a room next to their's."

"But I— Fine," said Claire with a sigh, crossing eyes with Michael, who in return shrugged ever so subtly.

"Alright, this meeting is dismissed. We'll meet on Tuesday, as usual."

"Sarah come on, the driver is waiting outside," noted Claire; Sarah nodded.

Sarah sat by the window side; sitting next to her was Michael. She grabbed a folded paper and slowly inserted in into Michael's pocket. Sarah then gazed upon the dimmed view outside the window.

Upon arriving, Claire got out first, and Sarah followed. Michael rushed to the bathroom; he locked the door, then unfolded the piece of paper, which stated: 'Meet me four hours from now.'

"What's going on?" wondered Michael. He then found a number written on the back of the paper; he saved the number, before texting Sarah.

"What's the meaning of this?"

"You'll know soon. Meet me outside the house in four hours; this way we can assure a private conversation," texted Sarah.

"Michael hurry, I have to use the toilet!" knocked Claire anxiously.

"Sorry, give me a sec…"

Michael flushed the paper then unlocked the door.

THREE HOURS LATER, Michael snuck outside the house. He found Sarah waving from the park on the other side of the road. "What are we doing here?" asked Michael, showing a serious tone.

"I'm here to talk some sense into you." Began Sarah, "How did you end up in this situation? To have no problems with killing your only sister?"

"I lost the only woman I ever trusted—the woman I opened my heart to. I then thought, what's the point of loving a mortal who'll leave when the opportunity presents itself? Such questions lead to me giving up on relationships..." Michael paused. "Well, until I locked eyes with her for the first time."

"You mean Claire?"

"I felt a strange feeling in my heart every time she would pass by me. I could see my dead friend in her. Humans are weak, especially when reminded of an old wound..."

"So, you gave up on your principles for her?"

"I lost control over my heart," remarked Michael.

"But why are you still with her? After knowing her truth, why didn't you leave her?"

"It was already too late. She killed Lucas's friend and served it for dinner!"

"Yeah, Claire told me about it. Must've been tough on you."

"I was afraid—confused. But Claire took me in, and I felt I belonged. It was a feeling I couldn't experience before, to belong to someone who knows my pain."

"You do know that killing and eating people is a crime, right? What if you got caught? You're throwing your life away for the sake of girl who sorta reminds you of your old girlfriend!"

"What about you, huh? You're even worse than me!" snapped Michael.

"I'll have you know that I was pulled into this mess against my will. You think I enjoy killing innocent girls? I do so because I'm one against three demons!" yelled Sarah.

"I thought you understood me, all of you. Turns out only

Claire did," Michael gave Sarah his back as he walked to the house.

"Wait, listen to this," Sarah pressed on the play button:

*"Dear Michael, it's your mother. How are you doing? I hope you're doing fine in Dubai. You know, your escape wasn't easy on me. And after your father died, I just feel that my purpose in life was sanctioned. I thought I was here to help my family. But that family disappeared, leaving a blind woman with her daughter. I'm sure you know the impact stress can have upon one's health. I know you are busy but listen to my final request: I trust you with Isabella, while I go to where your father is resting. Remember, if we ever failed you—if you ever felt that we disappointed you, just remember Isabella has nothing to do with it..."*

Michael faced Sarah once again; she could see his eyes tearing, "it's alright, let it all out."

"Lisa died?" muttered Michael. "How did you get this recording?"

"It doesn't matter. Though what does matters is that those 'evil parents' are gone now. So, let me ask you again, why are you still with Claire?"

Michael sat on the swing next to Sarah, "I-I don't know. I don't know what I'm doing now. My head feels heavy."

Sarah placed her hand on Michael's lap, "It's alright, Michael, don't lose hope. There is always a—"

"What are you saying? I ate girls and did drugs. What hope do I have?" snapped Michael.

"Can you reach Lucas?" he asked.

"Yeah, why?"

"Tell him to go back. Isabella can stay with David..." Michael stood up.

"Are you sure? Remember, you can't always run away."

"Damn it, now you're babbling Lucas's words! Well guess what, I'll run and run until I'm free—until I feel truly alive..."

"Well, well, well!" said Claire with a low tone. She peeked

through her curtains, which had a clear view from her room on the second floor. "Judging from how Michael reacted, I bet Sarah failed in whatever she tried to do. Too bad, Sarah, you're a bit late to help," Claire closed the curtains.

# BETRAYAL

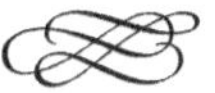



"Claire?"

"We have a small meeting, care to join?"

"A meeting? Where?" Michael grabbed his shirt off the floor and wore it.

"Oh, nothing special… The rest are waiting in the hideout," smiled Claire.

"Last time you said something like that, I saw my sister tied to a cross!"

"Relax, I promise it's nothing serious!"

Michael and Claire arrived at the hideout. As always, Michael went ahead, as Claire talked with Raul. "Here comes the traitor!" hissed Scarlett. Michael gave her a cold stare, then sat to the right of Claire's seat; facing him was Emily.

"Alright, we are all here! Let's start."

"Wait, where is Sarah?" inquired Michael.

"Now that you mentioned it, wasn't she with you guys?" noted Scarlett.

"She's still asleep. Apparently, she had a tough night. Am I right, Michael?" Claire shifted her eyes to Michael. He realized she knew what happened last night. He kept quiet and waited for Claire to see how much she actually knew.

"What happened last night?" asked Emily.

"Oh, I don't know! Why don't we let Michael indulge us?" the girls stared at Michael waiting for an answer.

"Sarah was so devastated by what happened to Jorge, she wanted me to leave—she thought I still have hope to return to my old life..."

"And what do you really want?" asked Claire.

"I want to stay here. What's the point of returning back to point zero?" answered Michael.

"There you have it, girls, Sarah is having second thoughts!"

"You know, it's been a while since we had a Middle Eastern girl!" remarked Scarlett.

"So, we're on the same page?" Both Scarlett and Emily nodded, while Michael thought about the risk he just placed on Sarah's shoulders.

"But how are we gonna do it? The girl's so skeptical. She's always careful and put ten possible scenarios for any given situation!" noted Emily.

"You got a point, but what if it was just a 'special dinner' for the five of us? I bet she would want to eat one more girl," schemed Claire.

"Sound's great! I'll start preparing the place for her," approved Scarlett.

"I'll help!" offered Emily.

"Now let's talk about the other threat: the one and only true threat—Lucas!" Claire switched to a more serious tone.

"Lucas is gonna pay. He almost killed ya!" remarked Scarlett.

"But we can't reach him," spoke Michael.

"Then I guess we could just ask Sarah," replied Claire.

Scarlett and Emily stood up and at once began preparing for tonight's special event. Michael grabbed Claire's hand before she could stand up. "Listen, you won't touch Lucas—or even Isabella for that matter. Got it?" he whispered.

"Why can't you accept the truth? They never loved you. These emotional attachments are just gonna kill you eventually," whispered back Claire.

"I'm warning you..." Michael tightened his fist around Claire's hands.

"Fine, I won't touch them." Michael took his hands off and returned to his seat. Claire's phone rang; she picked it, while still maintaining eye contact with Michael.

"Yello!"

"Where are you?" asked Sarah.

"We didn't want to disturb your jet lag. So Michael and I went to have breakfast. To be honest, the food was—let's just say that it was hard to digest..." Claire paused and winked Michael's way. "Anyway, been a while since we both went for dinner. How about tonight? The two of us?" offered Claire.

"What about Michael?"

"It's alright, I'm sure he'll understand." She glanced once again at Michael, who remained unmoved.

"Fine, I'll take your offer!"

"Excellent, we can go around six. In the meantime, go find you something to eat!" Claire hung up, and called the girls.

"Alright, here's the plan. You two will continue preparing for the dinner. Michael will join you later. And *I* will bring Sarah by six thirty." Explained Claire.

"Why don't Michael stay here and help us?" asked Scarlett.

"Sarah isn't dumb. She'll notice Michael's absence."

"Any other questions? Then let's get this over with!"

~

SARAH WENT to Lucas's hotel; she pushed on the doorbell and waited patiently. Isabella peaked through the tiny peephole. "Sarah? What are you doing at this time?"

"Is Lucas here?"

"No, he went for a walk," answered Isabella.

"Who walks in such weather? Never mind, Claire just called me."

"Isabella, you left the door opened—"

"Sarah?"

"Lucas, close the door and come have a seat," ordered Isabella.

"What happened last night? Did you talk to Michael?"

"I did."

"And?"

"He told me you guys should give up and head back to Dubai."

"Is he serious? Did he listen to that recording?"

"He just shed some tears. Though deep inside, I doubt he felt anything."

"Well I should've known that" sighed Lucas "I thought knowing that his mom was dead would move him a bit. But I guess Michael really cut himself loose from his parents."

"That's not everything," noted Sarah.

"What do you mean?"

"This morning, I awoke to an empty house. I called Claire. Turns out she and Michael went to eat breakfast alone. She also offered me dinner tonight—just the two of us," explained Sarah.

"You think she—"

"There is a big chance…"

"What are you gonna do about it?"

"You shouldn't go!" snapped Isabella.

"No, that will make Claire suspicious," remarked Lucas.

"You're right, I have to go. But do you… Back to Dubai."

"What are you saying? What about you?" snapped Lucas.

"Lucas, you almost killed her, she probably will try to take revenge—definitely!" noted Sarah.

"But—"

"I have an idea! Type your number here," spoke Sarah while tapping on her phone.

"What's that?" asked Lucas.

"This is an S.O.S app. But clicking on the power button in a pattern, I can send you a message with my location," explained Sarah.

"I see," Lucas took the phone and typed his number, then handed the it back.

"So here is how this will go down. I will go with Claire for dinner. If I didn't call you within two hours, well, I'm dead. And if I send you the S.O.S warning, it means I'm in danger. You then have to call the cops."

"Don't be pessimistic, Sarah," noted Isabella.

"I'm sorry Isabella, I must be prepared for everything."

"You got that, Lucas?"

"If you don't call, I'll assume you're dead. And if you send me an S.O.S, I'll call the cops. Got it!"

"When are you gonna go?" asked Lucas.

"Six or so…" Sarah walked to the door, "I'm sorry for putting you and Michael through all of this."

"Don't apologize, you did nothing wrong," smiled Lucas.

"It's almost one now, I have five hours left," thought Sarah as she was waiting for the elevator.

"You think she will be all right?" asked Isabella.

"If there is anything I've learned in the past few months is to have faith. Sometimes, you just have to rest knowing it's gonna be alright. Otherwise, you'll stress out over the slightest problem."

"Wow, never thought you were this wise…" joked Isabella.

"Well, life changes people. Whether you like it or not, you too will change—hopefully for the best!"

"You're a good man, Lucas." smiled Isabella.

It was 5:50PM, Michael was already at the warehouse. Sarah laid in the guest room, trying to process the events of tonight. She glanced at the recording device placed on the desk. "I almost forgot," thought Sarah. She took it the Michael's room, and hid it under his pillow.

"You're ready?" Claire knocked the already opened door.

"Yeah, let's go," smiled Sarah.

Claire called Raul to bring the car; she then waited outside alongside Sarah. Raul drove for ten minutes, Sarah realized they were getting away from the city.

"So, what restaurant are we going to?" asked Sarah.

"A well-known place—where it all started."

"They're here! Quickly, sit, sit!" remarked Scarlett as she peaked through the broken window. Michael and Emily took their places and awaited Sarah's arrival.

"Claire, what's going on?"

"Relax, they're just your old friends. Or did you forget them already?" Claire locked the huge metallic door and sat in her usual seat; Sarah stood in a defensive pose. "Why don't you have a seat?" offered Claire. Sarah nodded and sat next to Michael.

"So, where can you start, Sarah?"

"Depends on how much you already know."

"Hmm... let's say, EVERYTHING!"

"I felt that you lost faith in me after Jorge died. Is it because you still suspect me of killing him?"

"We both know you wanted him dead either ways," snapped Sarah.

"Then could it be because of Michael? Is that why you betrayed us?"

"Um, betrayed? Care to elaborate?" grinned Sarah.

"Let's see... How about 'oh Michael, you have to escape from here. Claire is crazy!' Does this ring a bell?" joked Claire. Sarah remained silent; she kept glancing at Michael, who tried to avoid any eye contact. "What do you have to say for yourself?"

"Nothing," replied Sarah.

"Hey, I bet you met Lucas. Care to share his whereabouts with your old friends?" requested Claire.

"Sorry, no can do!" smiled Sarah.

"Sarah, I've known you for a year now. You've always been a great help for me and the rest. BUT! We all know how this works..." remarked Claire.

"I do," Sarah reached for her pocket and pressed on the button three times. Scarlett was already reaching for a knife hidden in her bag. She handed it over to Claire, then grabbed Sarah from behind. Emily snuck under the table and held Sarah's legs tight.

"Michael, you have a life ahead of you. Choose your route wisely—"

"Goodbye, Sarah," Claire's knife had already pierced Sarah's neck.

"Boy it's been a while since I killed someone," chuckled Claire, unbothered by the stream of blood pouring underneath her. "Scarlett, Emily, clean up!"

Michael heard police sirens approaching. "COPS!" he snapped.

"What?" barked Claire.

"Sarah must've called them."

"But how? She was with us," inquired Scarlett as she tried to wipe her clothes.

"I bet she told someone about our plan. That's the only explanation," remarked Emily.

"Damn it, it's that night all over again!" muttered Scarlett.

"Any way, I'll go check on Raul, you keep cleaning up."

Raul heard the sirens and had already shifted the gears to 'D'. "Raul! Wait!"

"Are you crazy? I'm out of here!" Raul was already gone.

"Damn it, you coward!" yelled Claire.

"The driver's gone!"

"We're out of time, they'll surround the place any second now!" snapped Emily.

"Claire!" Scarlett threw a key towards Claire.

"Is that—"

"Don't waste any time! You and Michael go, and we'll try to manage."

"Are you crazy? They're the FUCKING cops!" cried Claire.

"Just go! Remember what I told you after killing your sister?"

"You would sacrifice your life for me," mumbled Claire. "Thanks Scarlett. You are a true friend!" Claire grabbed Michael's hand and rushed to the motorcycle.

"Scarlett, are you out of your bloody mind!" yelled Emily.

"You know, Claire was my first friend. Every day, my father would wipe my belly with a whip. He and his friends laughed as I bled. After he and his drunk buddies went somewhere else, I would go to Claire," Scarlett sat down on the floor, assuming a defenseless posture. "We all knew this day would come. Why not enjoy our last meal, hmm?" Scarlett grabbed her knife.

"I guess you're right. Claire did help me when the people around me left," sighed Emily, as she helped Scarlett slice

Sarah's hand. Each took a piece and ate their last meal together.

"God, she does taste good!" remarked Scarlett.

"Couldn't agree anymore!"

Both heard cars parking and footsteps approaching the main entrance. "Here we go…" whispered Emily.

"POLICE!"

"Stay safe, Claire…" mumbled Scarlett.

# AFTERMATH

LUCAS MADE SURE ISABELLA WAS IN BED BEFORE HEADING TO the location Sarah had sent him. It was the very same warehouse. He waved at a taxi and showed him the map, "Go to this place at once!"

"What's going on over there? I can't get any closer, sir," the driver stopped the car, as he approached a barricaded area with cops surrounding the circumference.

"It's my girlfriend... She's in danger!" Lucas immediately got off and went to the cops now eyeing him.

"Sir, this is a crime scene. Please step back."

"But it's my girlfriend. I'm the one who called you guys!"

"I'm sorry, but she's dead."

"Please, can I see her?" begged Lucas.

"She's right over there. Make it quick, will ya?"

"Thanks." Lucas hurried to Sarah who was lying on her back; her clothes were torn, and half of her right arm was gone. "Sarah!" Lucas tried to approach her body; he was stopped by the forensic team. By which then he took notice of two girls with white hair getting cuffed.

"It was him! He killed her!" Emily's desperate yelling was all she got at this point.

"It's over, Emily," whispered Scarlett.

"Sir, are you related to the victim?" asked the inspector.

"She's my friend," remarked Lucas.

"I'm sorry for your loss. If you don't mind, I have some questions."

"Sure," replied Lucas.

"Did you know anything about this?"

"To be honest, I had no idea my friend knew such people. We came here a week ago for our Christmas anniversary. I was going to propose tonight…" sobbed Lucas.

"Is that so? Next question, have you met those two lasses with white hair?"

"I believe Sarah spoke of them a couple of times. If I'm not mistaken, there is one more. I remember my Sarah frequenting them."

"Do you know any names?"

"I'm not sure. All I know is that they were a group of four, including Sarah. I was shocked the night Sarah met me with white hair. When asked, she said it was a 'thing' between them," explained Lucas as he wiped his fake tears.

"All right, we're gonna take it from here. Thank you for your time."

"Please avenge my girlfriend."

"We can't let a maniac roam the streets of London!"

"Um, if it's alright, I need a ride back to my hotel."

"Absolutely." Lucas walked behind the inspector to a police car parked within sight.

"Take this bloke to his hotel," he ordered.

"What's the address?" inquired the police officer as he closed the door on his side.

"Here you go," Lucas handed him the hotel card.

After arriving, Lucas saw Isabella waiting in the lobby with her sleeping dress on. "You're awake! I—"

"Where is she?" asked Isabella.

Lucas shook his head, "We were late." Isabella walked back to the room silently; Lucas followed her.

"Look, I know you're upset, but Sarah knew this would eventually happen to her."

"Why didn't Michael help her? If he knew she was in danger, why didn't he help her?" sobbed Isabella. Lucas hugged her; he knew it was too much for a 15-year-old girl to handle.

"It's almost nine, let's get some dinner. We'll go to that place you love!" Lucas placed a napkin in her hand. Isabella wiped her tears then went to the bathroom to change her clothes. "I'll wait in the lobby," he then left the room for Isabella to feel more comfortable.

"THEY'RE GONE! EVERYONE'S GONE!" yelled Claire.

"Scarlett sacrificed herself for us to escape," remarked Michael as he entered her bedroom. Claire was lying on her bed with both arms covering her tears.

"And all that for what? I failed as a leader—as a friend," sobbed Claire.

"I think it's time to stop," noted Michael.

"What's the point? My life is ruined…" sighed Claire.

"Look, as much as I'm against what we do, I don't think we should give up, not now at least. A new opportunity was presented to the two of us!" Michael sat next to Claire on the couch.

"What opportunity? They caught two members, you think they won't know about me? It's just a matter of time before this house gets ambushed."

"You know, I have an idea!" noted Claire, moments after terminating her preceding sentence.

"An idea?"

"Yeah! But I want you to keep an open mind about it."

"I'm listening…"

"Since our days are limited, why not live one last day together? A day neither of us will forget! We can get married, go to a love hotel— God, it's gonna be legendary!"

"Claire, you need to relax. You're stressed because of the girls," remarked Michael.

"What do you say? Shall we live one last memorable day?"

"Then what, HUH? After that day, what are we gonna do?" snapped Michael.

"I think we both know what's next… ending it all…" Claire reached for her small pouch.

"Wait, is that—"

Claire flicked the needle, then gave Michael a desperate smile. "Drugs aren't the answer!" the needle was already deep into her veins.

"Come on, we can start our legendary day from this moment!" smiled Claire. Michael sighed, then took the needle off her hands and inserted it into his left arm.

THE NEXT MORNING, Michael found himself on the floor. Beside him was Claire; her shirt was thrown on the couch, and her hands were covering her cold body. "Claire, wake up!" Michael grabbed the shirt and place it on Claire.

"M-Michael…" hesitated Claire.

"Come on, let's continue the best day of our lives!"

"What changed your mind?" asked Claire; she was dressing up as Michael tried to avoid looking directly at her.

"Growing up, I never had a perfect day. All my days were either studying or going with my father to boring events. Even after escaping, I feel that I'd lost a huge chunk of my lifespan. I just want to enjoy one day with someone I love!"

"I guess we both haven't enjoyed our childhood..." agreed Claire.

"What should we do first?"

"How about changing your hair style?" suggested Michael.

"My hair?"

"I bet they would keep an eye for any white-haired girl. You can dye it if you want," explained Michael.

"All right, what about you? What are you going to do in the meantime?"

"I'll be walking around."

"Fine, we will meet in that bridge. One hour from now."

Claire called a taxi, while Michael took a head start walking around town.

"Are there any hair salons nearby?" inquired Claire.

"I believe there is a woman-only one five minutes from here."

"That'll do!"

Claire handed seven pounds, all in coins. She pushed the entrance door and was welcomed by a receptionist, who stood behind a desk. "Hello, what can we offer you today?"

"I want a clean shave."

"Such charming hair! Are you sure about shaving it all?" Claire nodded slowly. "May I have your name?"

"Luna. Just Luna..."

"Very well, we shall call you. Please take a seat." Claire grabbed a magazine from the table, and sat at the waiting area.

"Ms. Luna."

"I wonder where Michael went," Claire strolled to the barber calling her name.

MICHAEL WAS WALKING AROUND, searching for a jewelry store. He tried asking some random passersby around him, before finally finding one. "Good morning, sir."

"Hi, can I see your engagement ring collection?"

"Here ya go," the old guy grabbed a ring set hidden underneath the counter.

"Do you have a one-of-a-kind ring? A *special* ring."

"Well we do have this ninetieth century Victorian ring. Twenty-four carat gold with an exquisite ruby crowned on top. I'm sorry, but what's your budg—"

"It doesn't matter. How much for the ring?" interrupted Michael.

"It's seven thousand quid, sir."

"I'll take it!"

"Would you like to pay using cash or credit card?"

"Um, credit card, please."

"She must be a special lady!"

"She is…" Michael tapped on the screen with his card.

"Would you like me to wrap the box?"

"No, it's all right," Michael took the ring box and stashed it in his coat pocket. "It's almost time!"

Michael tried to pace his walk to the promised location. He arrived at the same bridge he once confessed his love for Claire. On the other end was Claire heading for the same spot. "Michael!" she waved.

"Claire, your hair!" Michael took off his knitted hat and place it on Claire's head.

"I shaved it! I hope it didn't turn you off," chuckled Claire.

"You look beautiful with *and* without hair," Michael reached for the small box hidden in his pocket and took it out. He sat on one knee, while locking eyes with Claire.

"Claire, will you marry me?"

"Yes!" Claire hugged Michael.

People at once began clapping for the newly engaged love birds. Michael took the ring and slid it onto Claire's finger.

"It's beautiful!" sobbed Claire.

"Let's go get breakfast. We haven't eaten since yesterday!"

"I know a great place that serves brunch." Suggested Claire, to which Michael nodded.

"We'd like to sit outside."

"Please have a seat while I bring the menus," noted the waitress.

"This place looks great," remarked Michael.

"I used to hang with Scarlett here. Before I had to escape."

"Come to think of it, how come you escaped to Dubai?" inquired Michael.

"It was a Friday," Claire paused to take a sip from her orange juice. "We were preparing to meet this girl Emily knew. She'd betrayed Emily before, and we thought we would punish her! Scarlett and I approached her at a park, while Emily prepared the tools. We then invited her to a random house Emily found to see my 'hamsters'."

"What about the warehouse? Why didn't you just bring her there?"

"I couldn't risk blowing the hideout place. Plus, I'm glad we didn't take her there, because something unexpected happened. She had backup hidden in her car. The moment we showed out intentions. She yelled, and then we heard the door getting smacked by fists trying to force it open. Turns out she wasn't even the girl Emily knew!" Claire took another sip from her orange juice.

"I jumped from the back window, and so did Emily. We ran and eventually pumped into Jocelyn. From then, we decided to head for Dubai."

"Wait, what about Scarlett? Wasn't she with you?" asked Michael.

"Oh no, she had a bad case of fever and had to go home. She didn't witness the day we had there," remarked Claire.

"Anyway, we have a long day ahead. Let's go to the next place!" Claire tried to show a smile.

Michael paid the bill and walked with Claire to the tube tunnel. "Where to next?"

"How about a river cruise?"

"I bet we can find a private cruise for the two of us!" Michael placed his arm around Claire and pulled her to his side.

# TERMINUS

"What a day, huh!" Exclaimed Michael as he tried to catch his breath.

"Ya! Now we have to check in, then continue our magical night!" noted Claire.

"Where exactly is this hotel?" asked Michael.

"I'm not sure, but it has a view of Big Ben."

"Any names?"

"Um, the name..." Claire hastily checked the confirmation email. "HUED Hotel."

"Wait, I've seen that hotel before! It's over there," pointed Michael.

"Good evening sir, check in?" asked the receptionist.

"Yes, please."

"May I have the confirmation number?"

"Sure," Claire gave him the phone.

"All right... one night, am I right?" Michael and Claire nodded. "You also ordered the honeymoon package?"

"Honeymoon package?" inquired Michael.

"Yes, I thought since we *are* technically on a honeymoon, we might as well go all the way!"

"Here are your room keys. Enjoy your stay!" smiled the receptionist.

"It looks fancy!"

"The perfect way to end a perfect day!"

The room had candles scattered across the room. Soft jazz music was streaming from a phone attached to speakers. The bathroom had a small window with a view on the room. Right next to the bed was a huge window; both had a clear view of Big Ben. Michael laid down, as Claire went to take a quick shower. Michael's phone rang, it'd been a while since anyone called. He kept the phone ringing.

Moments later, the phone rang a third time; Michael walked to the table and picked up the phone. "Lucas?" thought Michael as he tapped on the answer icon.

"Hello?" whispered Michael.

"Michael! Isabella passed out in her room."

"What? What happened?"

"I don't know. I think she cried herself out. I was in the lobby, and when I came to check on her, she was lying still on her bed!"

"And why call me?"

"It's you sister for God's sake!" snapped Lucas.

"Listen, I'm busy—"

"NO, *you* listen! If you have any bit of empathy left in that heart of yours, you come to my hotel right now!" Lucas hanged up.

"Michael? Is everything all right?" asked Claire while untying her bathrobe.

Michael tried shaking the news off his head. He took three deep breaths, before locking eyes with Claire. "Everything is all right!" Michael forced a smile.

Claire took off her robe, "Come, Michael! Let's give this day the ending it deserves!"

"Nothing will ruin this night!" Michael assured himself as

he took off his shirt, tossing it away. "Not even the ignorant Isabella…" he muttered.

"First time?" teased Claire, and Michael nodded. "Same here," Claire lowered the volume as Michael tucked himself into bed.

~

"WOAH, that was awesome! Right?"

"I guess so…" hesitated Michael.

"What's wrong? Ever since I got out of the shower, you seemed a bit disappointed—more than usual," asked Claire.

"I'm just worried about what follows. I know it's hard to think about, but our lives are technically over. We have nothing to look forward to…"

"That's why we decided to have one last day. A day to fill in for all that happened," noted Claire.

"Now that you mentioned, today was indeed packed with some new experiences for me. I got engaged—that gotta count!"

"See, your life isn't meaningless. Now let us sleep before the grand finale!"

"How exactly are we going to do… the you know what?" inquired Michael.

"I was thinking we could go before sunrise. At the top of this hotel. We can watch one last sunrise together!"

"But it's gonna be hard to be 'invisible' with people walking around at that time," remarked Michael.

"Then how about four fucking AM?" suggested Claire.

"Yeah, that could work I guess."

"Now that everything is settled, I need to sleep. We had a long day, huh!" Claire wore back her robe, then switched off the lights.

Michael tried to close his eyes; his mind was busy

thinking about different stuff all at once. He wasn't sure whether to worry about his sister, or his own life. Michael finally gave up to his tired body and fell asleep…

"*Michael!*"

"*Anna! Is that you?*"

"*Look how things turned out. From a guy who wanted to be free, to someone who has lost hope in life. Is that what you wanted?*"

"*Anna, you don't understand, I—*"

"*And to think I risked my life to help you escape.*"

"*I don't know what happened to me. I thought I was doing the right thing, but then things got out of control. I ate Lyla and almost killed Isabella.*"

"*Michael, it's not too late to go back, for there never was any due date; that's the beauty of life!*"

"*How can you be so sure?*"

"*You wanna know why? Because I'm not real! This is just you talking with yourself! There wasn't any spirit whatsoever.*"

"*So, all these times, it wasn't you?*"

"*Exactly! This proves that you still have a part that hasn't given up yet…*"

"I—I—" mumbled Michael

"Michael! You're having a nightmare, wake up!" Claire shook his shoulder. Michael hurried to the bathroom and washed his face; he then took a minute standing before the mirror—observing what he had become.

"Is that even me?"

Michael then returned back to Claire, "Are you feeling better?" she asked.

"Yeah, sorry to bother you…"

Claire resumed her last sleep, as Michael struggled to have peace with himself. He then remembered that recording device he found under his pillow. Michael reached for his bag and grabbed the device out. He slid a pair of earphones connected to the recording device. Michael then walked to the window and pressed on the play button.

"Mom, I'm scared…"

MICHAEL HEARD Lisa's message again and again; until Claire's alarm rang. "Michael? Did you even sleep?" Claire wiped her eyes as she yawned. Michael turned toward Claire; in his face were traces of tears and soreness.

"Ready to do this?"

"Yeah, I'm ready," Michael wiped his face with his shirt.

Claire wore her pants and shirt. She attempted to stretch her upper body one last time. Michael, on the other hand, was waiting calmly by the window. His heart was racing like crazy, and his stomach wouldn't rest. "Time to go," Claire opened the door and looked both sides.

"Coming," Michael placed the recording device on his side of the bed, then exited the room.

Twenty floors later, both arrived at the 50th floor. The elevator's door opened, and they were facing a small staircase with a metal door at the end. Claire walked first and pushed the door open. Michael took one step at a time, as he found himself in the roof top. "It's chilly up here!" chuckled Claire; she then strolled to the edge, where she found an opening in the chainlink fence.

"You know, I'm glad they don't have these rooftop bars up here. Otherwise, the whole plan would've failed," yelled Claire in an attempt to reach Michael. She then stood on the edge on the hotel. London city was shining light beneath. Her eyes were locked on a landing spot down there. "Michael, the view's great!"

Michael finally arrived and stood near Claire.

"I wonder if anyone will miss me, or even remember that

I once existed as a member of this society," Claire closed her eyes. "I lived my childhood as a falsely labeled psychopath. And now, I'm living as a real psychopath who munches on girls—how ironic!"

"I never thought my life would end here. As a child, I always looked forward despite getting pulled back by my parents. After I came to Dubai, I thought this was my moment to shine; to be the man I wanted to be! And now, I am here," Michael started. "Anna was the only one who truly understood me. A person who did tamed the hatred in my heart. But after she died, I lost control over myself."

"But look on the bright side, you met me; a person who shared a fair amount of pain before. I know exactly what you are feeling because I also was betrayed by my family. At least yours didn't have enough courage to kick you out," Claire held Michael's right hand.

Michael gazed at her left hand holding his. A golden ring with a ruby on top was fixed in her finger. He then saw his life flashing right in front of him. Isabella, Lucas, and even Anna; Michael saw all those who mattered to him the most. He then raised his head and watched Claire; a girl who he met not even a year ago. Yet, she managed to turn his life. "Alright, on a count of three!" Claire tightened her grip on Michael's hands.

"This isn't right… My life isn't over yet. In fact, it barely started," thought Michael as Claire began counting.

"One…"

"Two…"

He slowly dejected his hands off Claire's grip.

"Th—"

Michael pushed Claire as he backed off the edge. "Michael! You son of a—" Claire landed on the sidewalk fifty stories below…

# INCEPTION

"I'm sorry Claire... I just realized the structure of life. We don't live to remember the past, we live to rewrite that past..." Michael rushed to Claire's corpse, he picked up her left hand and removed the ring off her finger. Michael then returned to the room and grabbed the note pad. He wrote a message addressed to Scarlett and Emily. It had some regret about Claire's life, and how she had betrayed them to escape. He then wrote her name in the lower corner of the page.

After packing his stuff, Michael went to the self-service kiosk located behind the reception desk. He checked out of the room under Claire's name, which she had used to check in. Michael had a scarf covering his lower face; and a cotton knitted hat covering his head. He ran past Claire's body with no destination in mind; running for three miles or so, before his body forced him to take a breath. Michael took his phone out to check the clock. He found one unread message from Lucas, it was a live location marking Lucas and Isabella's hotel.

Thus, Michael rushed to the sent location and walked into the hotel. "Hello sir, how may I help you?"

"Hi, I'm looking for my friend. He booked a room under Lucas Oskar," Michael showed him the map Lucas sent as a proof.

"Very well sir, he's in room eighteen o five. Please understand that I cannot give you a room key."

"I understand. I'll just call him to open the door. Thanks."

A group of tourists were blocking the two elevators. "This gonna take forever..." Michael glanced the stairs door. He opened the door and rushed through the floors. It took him fifteen minutes to finally reach the eighteenth floor. Michael looked left, then right in hopes to locate the room.

"There!" he carefully approached the door and pressed the small doorbell icon; but no one answered. He pressed it again, with no respond. Michael gave up and walked back to the elevator. The door was opened and a girl wearing a sleeping dress stood out.

"Michael!" she snapped.

"Isabella? I thought you—" Isabella jumped at Michael and hugged him. It was the first time she ever felt so happy to see him. Michael shared the same feelings as he hugged her back.

"Isabella, where did you go—"

"Michael?"

"Hey, Lucas..."

"Why are you here? And where is Claire?"

"Can I at least come in?"

"Of course!" laughed Isabella. Michael and Isabella entered the room. Lucas closed the door then joined them.

"So, what happened?"

"We were at the dinner table, waiting for Sarah to be served. Then, police ambushed the place. Claire and I managed to escape at the cost of Scarlett and Emily, they got left behind—"

"You do know I called the cops, right? Also, they questioned me, and I didn't mention you. I told them about Claire, and the other two girls," interrupted Lucas.

"We arrived at Claire's house, and she was lost. She had no idea what to do now that all her group are gone. Claire then proposed we have one last day together, before ending it. I was more desperate than her, so I agreed to live one last day. We got engaged, cruised around the city, and went to a five-star hotel."

"ENGAGED?" snapped Lucas; Michael took the ring out of his pocket and placed it on the table.

"It looks beautiful," Isabella took the ring and tried to wear it.

"Remember when I told you Anna came to me? Turns out it wasn't her, but something from my unconscious. By four, we were ready to end this perfect day. On the top of a fifty-story hotel we both stood; then I realized something. I scarified everything to escape from my parents. Why would I want to end things when they in fact just started going my way?"

"I'm glad you came back to your senses at the last moment. So did Claire—"

"I pushed her off the edge."

"I see…" said Lucas with a somewhat sad tone.

Isabella realized that Claire wore that ring she's holding and promptly placed it back on the table.

"I'm going back to LA with Isabella," spoke Michael.

"What!" snapped Isabella.

"Why will you go back?" asked Lucas.

"Lucas, you have a university to attend, and I doubt you could handle Isabella on your own," explained Michael.

"But still—"

"I'll ask James's family to take care of Isabella. That is, of course, if they agreed."

"Then what?"

"Then I guess I could return to the university. I think I still have a chance to pass this course."

"You know what, at least let me go with you guys to LA. I can risk skipping a class or two," begged Lucas.

"Fine…" sighed Michael. Lucas shifted his look to Isabella and smiled; she smiled back. "Lucas, cancel your flight, I'll book us a flight back to the US."

"You got it!"

"GOOD MORNING LADIES AND GENTLEMEN. As we start our descent, please make sure your seats and tray tables are in their upright position. Also, please make sure your seat belt is securely fastened."

"Isabella, wake up," Michael tapped on her lap. Lucas stood up immediately after the plane terminated by the gate.

"Let's go now," Lucas rushed to the flight attendance waiting by the door. Michael carried Isabella's backpack and stood up to make space for her to move. People started to open the overhead bin.

Waiting at the arriving hall was David. He waved at Lucas as he entered the hall. "Michael and Isabella, together at last!" David picked the luggage from Michael and Lucas.

"Sorry for making you go through this—all of you guys…" Apologized Michael.

"Where to now?" inquired David.

"James's house."

"Are you sure about it?"

"Yes, Isabella's gonna be fine with them," assured Michael.

"But I don't want to live alone there," said Isabella.

"Unless you want to live in an orphanage, you have no choice but to live with James."

The car parked in front of James's house. A butler

welcomed them, asking about their purpose of visiting. Michael got out of the car and asked to see James.

"Michael?"

"Good morning, Mr. James."

"What are you doing here? Haven't you done enough?" he snapped.

"I'm sorry for everything."

"Sorry? Sorry doesn't cover the fact that my only daughter married a guy I hated."

"Married?"

"After you escaped on the wedding day, Taylor brought home a guy claiming to be her fiancé. I tried to stop her, but she blamed you for not showing up. I lost my control over her because of your so-called rebellion."

"Is she home?"

"She left and went to live with her new husband," hissed James.

"Sorry for wasting your time, but do you know where I can find her?"

"No. And even if I did, I wouldn't tell you!" James marched back inside.

"Don't you have her number?" asked Lucas as Michael entered the car.

"You're right! Let me check," Michael searched through his contacts. "Found it!"

"Hello—"

"Michael? Is that you?"

"Hi, Taylor. How you've been?"

"Is everything all right?"

"Can I meet you? I have a favor to ask."

"You're in LA?"

"It's a long story."

"Any way, come to my house, I'll send over the location."

"Great, I'll see you soon."

"David."

"Alright," David took a glance at the address, then started driving.

"Lucas, I'm sorry for Lyla, guess they still haven't found her, huh."

"Michael, Emily told me everything. And I forgive you."

"I swear I had no idea it was her."

"What's important is that we moved on."

"Michael, we're here," noted David.

"Alright, let's go."

"Taylor?" Michael knocked on the door. Taylor opened the door and found Michael and the rest standing.

"Michael! Come in!"

"So, this is your new house."

"Yeah, although it's big for the two of us."

Taylor and the rest sat in the living room, while David stood near the door but was offered a seat on the couch.

"So?"

"I'm sure you've heard about this, but Lisa died."

"Yeah, I'm sorry for your loss."

"You see, I need to find another university, so I can't keep a close eye on Isabella."

"Actually, Paul and I were thinking of adopting," Taylor paused.

"Wait, does this mean—"

"I'm the problem… Although Paul, my husband, told me it's alright, I know that he always wanted a child or two," sobbed Taylor.

"Honey, I'm home," called Paul.

"In the living room."

"I brought—"

"What's going on?" Paul was on guard.

"It's alright," Taylor got off and hugged Paul.

"We're going to be parents!" she whispered.

"What! How?"

"There she is, our daughter to be!" Taylor pointed at Isabella.

"Hi, my name is Paul. Nice to meet you!" smiled Paul; Isabella tried to look away.

"So, what do you say? Will you keep an eye on my little sister?"

"Absolutely!"

"Isabella, can I see you for a moment?" Michael walked outside the house, and Isabella followed him.

"Listen, I know you might feel lonely, and I apologize. But believe me, Taylor is a nice woman. And remember, I'll always be around."

"I miss mom and dad…" sobbed Isabella.

"I know," Michael hugged his young sister; before she returned to her soon to be parents, "thanks for agreeing to be my parents," she said with a low tone.

"Of course, honey! We might not be Larry and Lisa, but we'll try our best to keep up with you," Taylor patted Isabella's head.

"I think it's time to go. We still have a lot of preparations to do," remarked Michael.

"See you soon, Isabella!" Paul waved as Isabella exited the house.

"David, home," ordered Michael.

After arriving, Isabella and Lucas got off. David was about to park the car when Michael stopped him. "David, I'm sure you know what's going on right now."

"You want to release us from our contract? Yeah, all the butlers know."

"Great. Anyway, thanks for your service the past, I can't even remember how long you worked here!" laughed Michael.

"I'm gonna miss you and Isabella."

"What are you gonna do from now on?" asked Michael.

"Maybe I'll travel the world…" smiled David.

"Is that so? Well, good luck wherever you go."

"So, this is your house," noted Lucas as he walked behind Isabella.

"Huge, isn't it?"

"What will happen to it?" asked Lucas.

"I have no idea. But I think Michael has something in mind," answered Isabella. "Feel free to roam around anywhere but my room!" Isabella entered her room and locked the door.

Lucas went to Michael, who had just walked into the mansion. "So, I guess that's it, huh!"

"Say, have you booked a return flight?" asked Michael.

"Um, no."

"Then why not stay a night or two here. I can give you my room," offered Michael.

"Two nights are too much. The most I can is one. After all I can't keep on missing classes," explained Lucas.

"Fine, then I guess you can return with me. I have some stuff to do here before returning though," remarked Michael.

"HI, ANNA. IT'S ME, MICHAEL…" Michael sat laying on his back on the back of the tombstone. "A lot has happened since I last saw you. Some happy moments, but mostly dark and sad. I thought I could find someone like you, someone who can replace you in the real life. Apparently, I wasn't ready to move on," Lucas sat next to Michael. He waited silently as Michael was talking to Anna's tombstone.

"I met a girl who almost ruined my life… That girl made me eat humans—can you imagine that! I even ate Lucas's girlfriend. I did drugs and all sort of stuff I thought would help me. As it turns out, I become lost rather than belonged. Lisa died and I didn't even shed a tear. My sister came seeking her brother's protection; yet I escaped to London when she has just arrived at Dubai."

"I don't think I can carry the pressure of all those I ate. They were little girls just starting their adulthood life. I took it away from them just like that. I'm sure you're wondering how all that ended. It wasn't easy. I had to—"

"Strange, I feel some—" Michael vomited all over Anna's grave.

"Michael! You alright?" snapped Lucas as he hurried to were Michael was, cutting short his stroll around the neighboring tombstones.

"I'm sorry… I don't know what's happening…" Michael apologized to Anna's grave.

"What's going on? My body is shivering, and I can't swallow very well," Michael recalled visiting Jorge's apartment. "The vomit… The night he met Claire… NO it can't be!"

"Michael?"

# ABOUT THE AUTHOR

Ivory Raven is the author of seven novels, including the 'A Desire' series, as well as the sub-series, 'A Desire: The Other Mischievous'.

# THE JOURNEY CONTINUES...

Founded in 2021, LJ Marshall's Publishing House solemnly believes in the quiet power of composed words—to stir minds, challenge norms, and echo through generations. We are devoted to publishing stories that defy the attenuated line between fiction and sanity—those that disturb, inspire, and linger long after the final page.